UNPLEASANT AWAKENING!

"Master?"

"Zzzzzz—what?" Lando blinked then stretched.

"Vuffi Raa, how many times have I told you never—"

"Master," the robot interrupted, sounding both worried and eager at the same time, "it's been nearly three hours. Have you come up with a plan?"

"Uh, not exactly. I'm working on it. I said I'd call you when—"

"Well, I think we'd better talk it over now. There's a picket cruiser sitting a hundred kilometers off our starboard bow. They've fired two warning shots already. Master, they say they'll cut us in half with the next shot unless we stand by to receive boarders."

Lando grunted. "That's the Centrality Navy for you, no consideration at all."

Also by L. Neil Smith
Published by Ballantine Books:

The Probability Broach

The Venus Belt

Their Majesties' Bucketeers

The Nagasaki Vector

Lando Calrissian and the Mindharp of Sharu

Lando Calrissian and the Flamewind of Oseon

Lando Calrissian and the Starcave of ThonBoka

A NOVEL BY
L. NEIL SMITH

BASED ON THE CHARACTERS AND
SITUATIONS CREATED BY GEORGE LUCAS

A Del Rey Book

BALLANTINE BOOKS • NEW YORK

A Del Rey Book
Published by Ballantine Books

Copyright © 1983 by Lucasfilm Ltd. (LFL)

Library of Congress Catalog Card Number: 83-90781

ISBN 0-345-31164-7

Manufactured in the United States of America

First Edition: December 1983

Cover art by William Schmidt

THIS ONE'S for F. Paul Wilson, Healer and friend, and for James P. Hogan, who makes seven.

ONE

Lehesu swam the endless Open Sea.

He was large for a young adult, although there were Elders of his species twice his size and mass. An alien observer in a different place and time would have pointed out his resemblance to an enormous manta ray—broad and streamlined, powerfully winged, and somehow pleasingly sinister. His sleek dorsal surface was domed high with muscle.

Others would have been reminded of the Portugese man-o'-war, seeing the tentacular ribbons hanging from his ventral side, marveling at the perfect glassy transparency of his body with its hints and flashes of inner color.

Yet, naturally enough, such comparisons would have been misleading. Lehesu had been born among the people who call themselves the oswaft. He was, unlike ray or jellyfish, penetratingly intelligent. Unlike most others of his kind, he was also aggressively curious.

He dwelt in a place the oswaft called the ThonBoka, which, in Lehesu's language, brought to mind visions of a cozy harbor on the margins of a stormy ocean. It was a haven of peace and plenty, a refuge.

◆ 1 ◆

There were those among the oswaft, principally family and friends, who had warned him smugly that he would regret adventuring beyond the safe retreat of the ThonBoka into the dark perils of the Open Sea. Few of them actually dared speculate precisely what those perils might consist of, what he might find, what might find him—except a quick, unpleasant death. For all their intelligence, the oswaft were not remarkably imaginative, particularly when it came to the topic of death. They were a long-lived people and patiently, even fatally, conservative in their outlook.

Others hadn't even cared enough to scold him. Lehesu, himself, was a nuisance and a danger, whose very presence was somehow inappropriate to the warm sanctum of the ThonBoka, a hint of the darker ugliness that lurked beyond its confines. To their credit, it would have been completely uncharacteristic of them to expel him, just as it would never have occurred to any one of them, regardless of personal opinion, to attempt to stop Lehesu from sacrificing himself to his incomprehensible exploratory itch.

At that moment, he was beginning to wish he had listened to *someone*. The Open Sea was slowly starving him to death.

He flapped his great manta wings reflexively to achieve calm. It was an awe-inspiring, majestic gesture—had there been anyone to see it—among his kind, the equivalent of breathing slowly and deliberately. And for Lehesu, it was every bit as effective: it didn't help in the slightest. If anything, it only reminded him that he *had* a plight to worry about.

He was not really frightened. For all their conservatism, fear came slowly to the oswaft, panic not at all. It was just that curiosity was not a common characteristic among them, either. They had their ancient, venerable, time-tested, firmly established, customary, and honored traditions. Such redundancy was necessary, Lehesu thought, to convey the suffocating stuffiness of it all. Yes, there were ways of accepting innovation. After all, his people weren't savages. It happened gradually, over several dozen generations. The culture of the oswaft was far from stagnant. It was simply excruciatingly boring.

Lehesu, on the other fin, was a genius of curiosity—or a totally demented mutation. The conclusion depended on whom you sought for an opinion, Lehesu or any other individual of his species. In his thirst to know what un-looked-for wonders lay beyond the cloying safety of ThonBoka, he was utterly alone. He could not so much as begin to explain the burning need that drove him into the Open Sea—not to anyone his own age, certainly not to any of the Elders, no, not even to the younger ones.

Well, perhaps one day he would have young of his own. And if curiosity were something that could be passed on, they would understand and share his thirst. He chuck-led to himself: how he would ever find a mate who could tolerate him might constitute something of a problem.

Then again, it might not. It was highly unlikely he would survive traversing what amounted to a desert. Every fiber in his great and graceful body ached with hunger. He had been cruising for what seemed an eternity without encountering a molecule of nutriment, and it was far too late to go back. He lifted his enormous wings once more, unable to ignore their rapidly failing strength.

Lehesu had never seen or even heard of a cat, but he would have understood what killed it, how, and why. Still, he couldn't really bring himself to regret what he had done. Curiosity may have killed him already, but it was vastly better than dying from boredom.

Perhaps.

Lehesu estimated that he had, at most, only a few

hours before he expired. His people fed continually as they moved about through life, automatically, almost unconsciously. There was little capacity in his gigantic body for storage of nutrients. As he weakened, and the effect was increasingly noticeable, increasingly painful to him, he reflected that at least he was dying in the Open Sea, away from all the—

But wait! What was that? There was something else in the desolation! Far beneath him in the depths, another entity swam, one that pulsed with life and power. Stretching his sensory abilities to their limit, he could feel that it was comparatively tiny, yet it virtually sang with strength—which meant there had to be sustenance around somewhere.

He did another uncharacteristic thing then, something no other oswaft would have done: he dived for the object. Lehesu was not a predator. Nor was he herbivorous. Such distinctions had no meaning in his time and place, under those circumstances. It was the habit of the oswaft to eat whatever they found edible, leave everything else alone. They knew of no other intelligent species, and the entirety of creation was their dinner plate.

At least he could discover what the thing had found to eat. He realized there was a possibility that it would find *him*, and he had little strength for fighting left, even if he had been inclined to fighting, which he was not. Yet he had less hope, even, than strength.

Down and down he went. Yes, there it was, a mote less than a tenth his size, yet he could feel that it was stronger than he was by a substantial margin. Better armored, as well, much like the small carapace-creatures that swam the calmer currents of ThonBoka.

They were delicious.

As he approached the thing, he could see that it was not shaped terribly differently from himself. To judge from its direction of travel, it was a bit broader than it was long, more rounded in its major contours than he was. Like Lehesu, it had two nondescript projections on its frontal surface, although whether they were sensory arrays, like his, was another question.

Lehesu's senses were not strictly limited to straight lines. He could "see" that the creature possessed no manipulators on its underside. He had hundreds. Yet it appeared that part of the surface was capable of opening; perhaps its tentacles folded into its belly. He knew of organisms that—

Lehesu recoiled in shock! He was near enough now to make out and be astounded by a major difference between himself and the . . . the thing. It was completely *opaque*, like a corpse! His people lost their transparency upon dying and, until they decomposed into the dust of which all life is made, remained visually impenetrable. This creature looked like a dead thing, yet moved with confidence and fleetness. There were those among his people who . . . But Lehesu was not superstitious. With a mental snort, he rejected such foolish notions. Almost completely.

Another, milder surprise awaited him. Drawing even nearer—any other oswaft would have known then and there that Lehesu was quite insane—he felt the thing trying to say something. The ThonBoka was vast and its people many, but neither so vast nor numerous that separate languages had ever developed. Within their limits, the oswaft were far too wide-ranging, too swift. And they could speak over distances that would only seem incredible to many another race.

And so he felt the tingling of communication, for the first time in his life without being able to understand it. He broadcast a beacon of good wishes himself and waited.

His own message was repeated back to him. He repeated the first greeting the small armored creature had sent him.

Each now knew the other to be an intelligent organism. That was as far as communication could proceed. The armored creature began counting—that was silly, thought Lehesu; if it were intelligent, of *course* he could deduce that it would be able to count. Thinking hard, he spoke a picture-message, one meant to convey visual reality rather than pure ideas. Lacking any better image, the wave front he transmitted was that of the small armored object before him.

A rather long pause followed. Deep within Lehesu, he experienced a brief sensation of satisfaction that *he* could surprise *it*. Then he received a picture-message of himself. Fine! Now he could convey the essence of his disastrous situation to it, and perhaps it would help him. If in no other way, perhaps it could help pull him into richer currents.

He spoke a picture of himself, then modified it in his imagination until he showed a pitiable scene in which he was growing increasingly opaque, increasingly withered. Finally, just to do things properly and in full, he imagined himself dissolving, his molecular constituents wafting away. It made him feel very strange to imagine such a thing, but it was necessary.

Finally, he started the image over again, but this time had himself feeding richly on what drifted in the currents of ThonBoka. He pictured himself growing stronger, healthier, sleeker, more transparent. He pictured himself growing to become a giant Elder. For some reason this made him feel worse than did the idea of dying, although whether the feeling came from imagining a feast while he was starving, or imagining himself in the image of his stuffy forebears, he was not quite certain.

In any case, the creature hung motionless before him

in the void, nor did it reply for a long, long time. As he waited, Lehesu examined it carefully. Numerous spots glowed on its outer surface, much like the courting glow pigments of some of the ThonBoka wildlife. One in particular, a large globular spot at the front end, displayed odd, changing patterns. All the while, the creature pulsed and throbbed with indecently good health. It had come to a halt when the communications began, and continued to be still though obviously restless and thrumming to be on its way.

Finally, it sent him a picture-speech. That caught him by surprise, as his mind had wandered—another dangerous sign of imminent starvation. He had been gazing at the stars, wondering what they were, how far away they lay, and how he might, if he lived, contrive to reach them, as he had reached the Open Sea.

The armored creature asked him, in effect, if *these* were what he liked to eat. It then began displaying pictures of every imaginable variety of wonderfully delicious nutriment, from the incidental nutrient haze that drifted on the currents and was gobbled up by oswaft as they passed, to the most succulent of complex culinary creations. The trouble was, these images were mixed incomprehensibly with things he didn't even remotely recognize—and with downright garbage.

Excitedly he shouted confirmation when the images were right, withheld comment when they were not. He and the creature hadn't gotten around to establishing the symbols for "yes" and "no". He wondered what the thing had in mind. Would it lead him to this banquet it was promising? Would he have the strength to follow? Or was it merely mocking him?

He was beginning not to care. There were only minutes left for him, anyway.

Suddenly, the greatest shock of all. The belly of the

creature split open and vomited out everything it had shown him. It filled the currents around them, forming an almost impenetrable fog. Shouting joyously, he swooped and dived and soared through it all, plowing great clean swaths where he had passed. The creature stood off, watching, doing, and saying nothing.

One pass took him very near the thing. It was not smooth but was covered with knobs and bulges. Only portions of the thing showed any signs of transparency, and they simply admitted the sensory probes into an internal darkness that revealed nothing.

But for once, Lehesu's curiosity was abated. He fed, perhaps more richly than he ever had in his life. Each pass brought him nearer the creature, but he was not afraid of it; it had saved his life. His senses passed over a spot that might have told him a great deal more, except that the oswaft had no written language, no need for one. It was a plate, a plaque, attached with rivets to the creature's hide. On it were enameled five words that would have shocked him deeply, for this was not a living creature at all.

The sign read:

MILLENNIUM FALCON
Lando Calrissian, Capt.

Lehesu the oswaft, swimmer of the starry void, was content merely to soar and graze about the *Falcon*, singing out his gratitude to her every second he did so, with the natural radio waves generated by the speech centers of his mighty brain.

The formaldehyde was *delicious*!

TWO

Lᴀɴᴅᴏ Cᴀʟʀɪssɪᴀɴ, ɢᴀᴍʙʟᴇʀ, ʀᴏɢᴜᴇ, sᴄᴏᴜɴᴅʀᴇʟ— and *humanitarian*?

It didn't seem very likely, even to him. But the un- deniable truth was that, several months after her initial encounter with that remarkable spacebreathing being, Lehesu of the oswaft, circumstances found the *Millen- nium Falcon* stolidly boring her way through the inter- stellar void straight toward the ThonBoka, which translated roughly into human languages as the Starcave.

Lehesu's people were in trouble: Lando was bringing help.

He *was* the help, and he was furious. His anger had nothing directly to do with Lehesu, the oswaft, *or* the ThonBoka, but was rather more closely connected with the broken arm he was nursing at the moment. It was not quite so onerous nor prolonged an ordeal as it might have been in a more primitive place and time. He wore a complex lightweight brace consisting of a series of electrical coils that generated a field that would encourage his fractured humerus to knit up nicely in two or three days. Yet the appliance was cumbersome and inconvenient, particularly in free-fall. And Lando had grown particularly fond of free-fall. It helped him think.

With the deck-plate gravity switched off, he would sit in the middle of a room—equidistant not only from its walls, but from its floor and ceiling as well—parked comfortably on a cushion of thin air, cogitating. But the cast got in the way.

Lando also had a black eye and a broken toe. But, considering everything else that had happened, those were minor annoyances. He flicked expensive cigar ash at a vacuum hose he'd arranged to hang conveniently nearby, and spoke in the direction of an intercom panel set in a table somewhere beneath him.

"Vuffi Raa, what's our ETA again?"

The instrument returned a voice to him, soft-spoken and polite, fully as mechanical in its origins as the instrument itself, yet rich with humorous astute inflection.

"Seventy-six hours, Master. That's a new correction: this region is so clean we've gained another four hours since I made the last estimate. I apologize for my previous inexactitude."

Inexactitude! Lando thought. The Core-blessed thing talks prettier than I do, and *I'm* supposed to be the con *artiste* around here!

The *Millennium Falcon*'s velocity, many times greater than that of light, was limited only by the density of the interstellar medium she traversed. Ordinary space is mostly emptiness, yet there are almost always a few stray molecules of gas, sometimes in surprisingly complex chemical organization, per cubic kilometer. Any modern starship's magnetogravitic shielding kept it from burning to an incandescent cinder and smoothed the way through what amounted to a galaxy-wide cluttering of hyperthin atmosphere. But the resistance of the gas was still appreciable through a reduction in the ship's theoretical top speed.

The particular area the *Falcon* was then passing through seemed to be an exception. Bereft of the usual molecular drag, the *Falcon* was outdoing even her own legendary performance.

The captain pondered that, then addressed the intercom again. "Better back her off a few megaknots. I need more time than that before this confounded dingus comes off my arm. And you've still got a dent or two yourself that needs ironing out. And Vuffi Raa?"

"*Yes, Master?*" was the cheerful reply. Lando could hear the clack-clack-clack of keyboard buttons being punched as per his instructions. The vessel slowed, but that could not be felt through her inertial dampers.

"Don't call me master!"

That had been very nearly reflexive. He'd long since given up wondering what the robot's motivation was for the small but chronic disobedience. Actually, Lando was concerned about his little mechanical friend, and not just because Vuffi Raa was such a terrific pilot droid. Or at least not entirely. These sporadic violent attacks they'd been suffering lately were getting to be a serious matter where they had only been minor nuisances before, and knowing *why* they were happening, to Lando's great surprise, hadn't helped a bit.

The gambler sneered down at his foot where another, tinier set of coils pulsed healing energies into his flesh. Somehow, *that* was the final insult—that and the black eye. It was one thing to attempt to murder an enemy. That was what a vendetta was all about, after all. But to do him in by millimeters, an abrasion here, a contusion there? Fiendish, Lando was forced to admit—if it wasn't simple ineptitude. Somehow the enemy realized that a man otherwise willing and capable of barehandedly confronting a ravening predator his own size, sometimes panics at the sound of a stinging insect barnstorming around his ears.

Well, the gambler told himself, that's why we're on this so-called errand of mercy. I'm going to put a twelve-gee stop to all of this juvenile assassination nonsense, one way or the other, once and for all.

Sure, it was a risky proposition; the stakes were as high as they could be. But above and beyond every other consideration, Lando Calrissian—he told himself again—was a sport who'd wager anything and everything on the turn of a single card-chip.

That's how he'd gotten into the mess in the first place.

It seemed that, some time before, a talented but essentially prospectless young conscientious-objector-of-fortune had won himself a starship—actually a converted smuggling freighter—in a game of seventy-eight-card *sabacc*. A little while later he had, quite unintentionally, acquired a pretty peculiar robot in much the same fashion. Together, the two machines and their man had set out upon a series of adventures, some more profitable than others. In the process, they had made a number of enemies, one of them a self-proclaimed sorcerer who had plotted to Rule The Galaxy, and had tripped over Lando on his way to the top. Twice.

The fellow had resented that, blamed Lando for his own bumbling and bad luck, and the vendetta had begun. Until now, it had been an unrequited, entirely one-sided relationship. All Lando wanted was to be left alone. He'd tried explaining, via various media, that he didn't care who ran the universe—he'd break whatever rules it suited him to disobey in any case, whoever was in charge—and that the sorcerer was perfectly welcome to all the power and glory he could grab. Alas, these blandishments, reasonable as they sounded to the gambler, had fallen upon inoperative auditory organs.

Just to make things really complicated, Vuffi Raa had already had enemies of his own. Although the robot hadn't known it. His previous master, while spectacularly untalented at games of chance, had been a highly effective government employee in the spy business. This fellow ostensibly an itinerant anthropologist, had used the little robot, forced him to help undermine a previously undiscovered system-wide civilization in a manner that had resulted in the brutal military extermination of two-thirds of its citizens. The remaining third, understandably perturbed, had sworn eternal hatred for the droid, and had enthusiastically begun to do something about it.

Subsequent attempts at negotiation, as in Lando's case, had been nearly lethally futile. Some people just won't listen.

Well, life is like that, Lando thought as he hovered in what had been designed as the passenger lounge of the *Millennium Falcon*. It served as their living room; just then, it was the gambler's private thinking-parlor, and the thoughts he was thinking were reasonably ironic. He took another puff on his cigar.

The trouble with two partners having separate sets of mortal enemies is that said enemies don't always make distinctions. Particularly when using fragmentation grenades. Poor Vuffi Raa had gotten badly dented by an assassin in the employ of the sorcerer at their last port of call. The idiot had confessed before expiring; with the nervousness of a beginner, he'd thrown the pin instead of the grenade. The robot's injuries would work themselves out after a while. He had excellent self-repair mechanisms.

In another incident, Lando had been pushed over a rail into a vat of vitamin paste he had considered acquiring for that very trip, somehow fracturing both arm and toe and picking up a shiner. What really hurt was that he'd simply *ruined* his second-best velvoid semiformal captain's uniform. He was certain Vuffi Raa's enemies were responsible. It felt like their style. Clumsy.

Nor was the *Millennium Falcon* considered immune. In fact, she'd rather taken the brunt of things, with bombs planted inside her (two of which had actually gone off) and having felt the fury of several small space battles in recent months. A fighter pilot had deliberately rammed her, crumpling her boarding ramp. She'd strained her engines getting them in and out of various places in a hurry. Her battery of quad-guns, under Lando's capable direction, had staved off the occasional pirate vessel, who probably hadn't anything at all to do with vendettas. Surprised at the ferocity with which her captain had taken it all out on their hides, defeated pirates were giving the battered old freighter quite a reputation.

Pirates they could handle. The *Falcon* was a good deal faster than she looked, terrifyingly well armed; he and the robot were pretty hot pilots, but Vuffi Raa had taught Lando everything he knew in this regard. Lando told himself again that the business at the Starcave would pay off all other debts, as well. He was thoroughly fed up, loaded for whatever furry omnivorous quadruped the fates cared to place in his path.

Tugging gently at the vacuum ashtray hose, Lando drifted to the ceiling of the lounge, gave a little shove against the overhead, which propelled him near the floor. He switched on the gravity and walked both forward and starboard around the *Falcon*'s curving inner corridor, to the cockpit, which was set in a tubelike construction projecting from the front of the ship.

In the left-hand pilot's seat, an equally weird construction perched, a five-limbed chromium-plated starfish with a single glowing red eye set atop its pentagonal torso. Its tentacles were at rest just then, having reduced the *Falcon*'s speed as Lando had requested.

The meter-high entity turned to its master. "I believe you'll be able to make out the nebula now, Master. See, that blurry spot ahead?"

Lando strained his eyes, then gave up and punched the electronic telescope into activation. Yes, there it was: the ThonBoka, as its inhabitants called it. It was a sack-shaped cloud of dust and gas, enterable only from one direction, rich with preorganic molecules even up to and including amino acids. Inside that haven, life had evolved without benefit of star or planet, life adapted to living in open empty space. Some of that life had eventually acquired intelligence and called itself the oswaft. But at the moment, they were under seige.

"What about the blockade, can you locate that?" Lando strapped himself into the right-hand seat, ran a practiced eye over various gauges and screens, relaxed, and plucked a cigar out of the open safe beneath the main control panel.

"Yes, Master, I'm overlaying those data now."

Vuffi Raa's tentacles flicked over the panel with a life of their own. He was a Class Two droid, with a level of intelligence and emotional reaction comparable to those of human beings. He had a good many other talents, as well. To Lando's occasional disgust, however, the robot was deeply programmed never to harm organic or mechanical sentience, and was thus an automatic pacifist. There had been times when that had been inconvenient.

On the main viewscreen, showing the sacklike ThonBoka nebula, a hundred tiny yellow dots sprang to life.

Lando whistled. "That's quite a fleet for bottling up

one undefended dust cloud. What do they think this is, the Clone Wars?" He leaned forward to light his cigar, but was stopped by the offer of a glowing tentacle tip. Yes, Vuffi Raa had a lot of useful talents.

"That isn't even half of them, Master. Although I can't understand why, some of the fleet out there have modified their defense shielding into camouflage to conceal themselves. I also believe they've mined the mouth of the nebula."

Puffing on his cigar, Lando forced calm. "And we're going to run that blockade. Oh, well, it's been a short life but a brief one. Can you do anything about shield camouflage for us?"

The robot wiped the screen display. "I'm afraid not, Master, it's very sophisticated technology."

"Which means that everybody in the universe is using it except civilians. Well, then, what's our plan?"

There was a startled pause that might have been filled with a blinking red eye had Vuffi Raa been capable of such a thing. "I thought *you* had the plan, Master."

Lando sighed resignedly. "I was afraid you'd say that. To tell the truth, I had a plan, but it seems pretty insubstantial, here and now. I shall repair to my free-fall cogitorium once more and reconsider. I'll get back to you as soon as possible. Don't hold your breath, it may very well be a century or three."

He unstrapped himself from his chair, took a final disgusted look through the sectioned canopy, and removed himself from the control area with his cigar. Around the long, heavily padded corridor, out into the cluttered lounge, off with the artificial gravity, and back to the geometric center of the room, where he sat and smoked and tried to think.

It wasn't one of his better days for that.

"Master?" The voice coming over the intercom was agitated. It startled the gambler out of a dream in which, no matter what *sabacc* hand he held, his cards kept changing to garbage, while a faceless gray opponent held a newly invented one, the Final Trump, which was an automatic twenty-three.

"Zzzzzz—what?"

Lando blinked, discovered that he was covered with sweat. His velvoid semiformals were soaked through, and he smelled like a Bantha someone had ridden half to death. He stretched, trying to remove kinks from his muscles that shouldn't have been there in zero gee.

"Vuffi Raa, how many times have I told you never to call me—"

"Master," the robot interrupted, sounding both worried and eager at the same time, *"it's been nearly three hours. Have you come up with a plan?"*

"Uh, not exactly," the gambler replied, shaking his head in an unsuccessful attempt to clear it. "I'm working on it. I said I'd call you when—"

"Well, I think we'd better talk it over now, if you don't mind. You see, there's a picket cruiser sitting not more than a hundred kilometers off our starboard bow. I didn't see them, so well camouflaged were they, and they've fired two warning shots already. Master, they say they'll cut us in half with the next shot unless we stand by to receive boarders."

Lando grunted. His mouth tasted like a mynock cave. "That's the Centrality navy for you, no consideration at all."

THREE

CONCEALED BEYOND THE REACH OF CIVILIZATION LAY A place called Tund, a name of legendary repute, one seldom spoken above a whisper. That whispered word named a planet, a system, or a cluster of stars—no one was quite certain which—rumored for ten thousand years to be the home of powerful and subtle mages. Fear was associated with the name, the sort of fear that inhibits mentioning, even thinking about, the thing it represents, so as not to invoke its omniscient, omnipotent, and malevolent attention. Almost no one knew the even more hideous truth.

The planet Tund was sterile, devoid of native life, its surface roasted to a fine, gray, powdered ash where evergreen forests, tropical jungles, and continent-broad prairies had once stretched for countless kilometers. It was a world destroyed by magic.

Or by belief in magic.

At night the planet's face glowed softly, not merely with the pale blue fire of decaying atoms, but with a ghostly greenish residue of energies as yet unknown to the rest of galactic civilization. Where it flickered balefully, nothing lived, or ever would again. It had been partially to preserve the secret of such power that Rokur Gepta, last of the fabled Sorcerers of Tund, had utterly obliterated every living thing upon the planet, from submicroscopic wigglers to full-flowering sentience. His was a terrible, cosmically unfeeling precaution.

The rest had been sheer malice.

Here and there an oasis of sorts had been permitted its closely regulated probational existence, areas reseeded from which, some billions of years hence, when the evil emerald fires had at long last died, life might resume its pitiably humbled march. Massive force-fields were essential to press the flickering death away from those few havens.

In one such crouched the Centrality Cruiser *Wennis*, a decommissioned, obsolete, and thoroughly effective instrument of pitiless warfare, being refitted to her master's precise specifications. Her crew was an odd but deliberate mixture of the cream of the galaxy's technical and military elite and its dregs, often represented in the same individual. Her weaponry and defenses ran the gamut from continent-destroying hell projectors to small teams of unarmed combat experts. She had been a gift of prudence from the highest and consequently most vulnerable of sources in the galaxy.

The *Wennis* would not be recognizable when Rokur Gepta was through with her.

The sorcerer had that way with ships, and planets, and people. The only value anything possessed for him was its utility relative to his inexorable rise to power. Wealth meant nothing more to him than that, nor the companionship of his fellow beings, even—owing to the most peculiar and repulsive of physical circumstances—that of females. He was empty, as devoid of life and warmth as his handiwork, the planet Tund itself. Such an emptiness requires endless volumes of power to fill it even momentarily.

Someday he, too, would bestow gifts of decommissioned battle cruisers—although he would exercise considerably more care to see that they were employed strictly in his interests. And even *that* lofty seat of power was only a feeble beginning. The million-system civilization ruled from it, after all, was only a small wedge of the galaxy.

And the galaxy itself only a small part of . . .

Deep within the twisted caverns of the murdered planet Tund, where Rokur Gepta had once personally searched out and exterminated every one of his ancient mentors— the original sorcerers, who had lovingly instructed him in the ways of power that had been their ultimate undoing—the treacherous former pupil sat, immersed in thought. He brooded in a blackness utterly unbroken by the glimmer of so much as a single passing photon. That was the way he preferred it; he had other means of observing reality.

Even in the full light of a healthy planet's daytime surface, another individual would be less fortunate: Rokur Gepta was simply impossible to come to terms with visually. He was a blur, a vagueness more psychological than perceptual in character, perhaps because his color was that of terror.

On the very rare occasions he was spoken of by others, descriptions varied: he was a malignant dwarf; a being of average though preternaturally imposing stature; a frightening giant of a figure over two meters tall, perhaps three. All accounts agreed that he was perpetually swathed in cloaks and windings of the same hue as his lifeless domain, an ashy gray from the tips of his (presumed) toes to the top of his (apparent) head. He wore a turbanlike headdress whose final lengths were wound around the place his face should be, obscuring all his features save the eyes, twin pools of whirling, insatiable, merciless voracity.

Understandably, the sorcerer had enemies, although he had outlived—often by design—the small minority of them with the capacity to do him harm. He had outlived many others as well, simply by surviving centuries of time. His long life was in grave and constant danger, however, from those few who still survived and the continually fresh crop of victims who wished him ill. And that was what produced his quandry.

Word had been conveyed, through several layers of underlings, of an emissary, a messenger whose credentials offered a potentially profitable alliance. Should he trust the individual sufficiently to hear him out, as per request, in total privacy?

The sorcerer pondered. The risk of a personal audience was great, especially as the representative came from a principal powerful enough to preclude extensive security measures, which could be interpreted as an affront. There were limits to the precautions that could be taken, but none to the cleverness of assassins. He ought to know; he had employed enough of them himself.

Reaching a decision, he gestured with a gray-gloved hand. Feeble light began to glow within the monstrous cavern, swelling until it filled the place. Small black hairy things within the walls squeaked a protest, rustled in their niches, then settled back into troubled somnolence.

He would make up this discomfort to his pets, Gepta thought, and if the audience turned out to be less than advertised, so would the emissary make restitution, most slowly.

A faint electronic chirp from a panel in the left arm of his basaltic throne alerted him of visitors. He firmed up his visual appearance; no sense alarming the messenger unduly at the outset. The time for intimidation, confusion, and betrayal would come later. It always did.

From a passageway far to the right, across a kilometer or more of cavern floor, a small procession wended its way, composed of minions in Centrality uniform, their marks of rank and organization stripped away to preserve the fiction that they were civilians. In truth, they were the same sort of gift the *Wennis* had been, and served their original master by serving Rokur Gepta.

The honor guard consisted of a half-dozen heavily armed and smartly groomed beings, every fiber bristling at attention as they marched. In their midst was a giant, a large, heavyset man in a battered spacesuit, carrying his helmet under one arm. The group wound carefully among the cavern floor's many stalagmites, following a hidden pattern that, if strayed from, would precipitate their immediate and total destruction.

Gepta waited on his throne, three meters above the floor.

As the column reached its base, Gepta's soldiers snapped to a halt. The visitor technically stood at attention, too, but he was the sort of being who, when the time came, would look as if he were lounging indolently in his own coffin. He was utterly relaxed, utterly alert. He was utterly unafraid of anything, most especially death.

If Rokur Gepta feared anything himself, it was men such as this.

"Sir!" the leader of the guardsmen said, "we present Klyn Shanga, Fleet Admiral of the Renatasian Confederation, sir!"

Gepta would accept no title or honorific. Such were for lesser beings. He tolerated being called "sir" because his underlings, of military background, seemed to grow increasingly uncomfortable and uninformative unless they could insert it at least once in every sentence they addressed to him.

Gepta nodded minutely, looking down on the craggy giant. "Admiral, welcome to the planet Tund," he hissed. "Few have seen it, save my minions, and even fewer have lived to say they've seen it."

Shanga grinned broadly from a face that was one scar overlaid upon another until nothing of the original flesh remained. Yet an ordinary human being would have found the effect somehow pleasing. Klyn Shanga was everybody's adventurous uncle, the one who'd been everywhere, done everything, and had it done back to him.

He ignored the threat: "That 'Admiral' is something in the nature of a joke, Sorcerer. In Centrality terms I'm more of a squadron leader, and it's not much of a squadron. Core—for that matter, it's not much of a Confederation, either! But we have our points, as my letters of introduction demonstrated, I'm sure. You know about the Renatasia?"

Gepta nodded once again. Upon receiving the communication in question, he'd consulted references and had a conference with his kennel of Centrality spies. What was to be learned was skimpy; there had been a highly energetic cover-up. Yet the essential facts were clear.

"It was a system and a culture colonized long before the current political status quo was achieved. It developed independently, unknown to the rest of the galaxy, and at a somewhat slower pace technologically. It was discovered, subverted, exploited, and obliterated by certain commercial interests acting in concert with the Centrality navy. You, your squadron, and your Confederation are some of the rare survivors. Are these the fundamental elements of the story, Admiral Shanga?" The sibilance of Gepta's whisper echoed in the cavern.

Shanga's turn to nod. "That's it. About a third of the population lived, reduced further by starvation and disease." He leaned against a stalagmite, casually swinging his helmet by a strap around his finger. "Get rid of the flunkies and we'll talk a deal, how about it?"

Gepta savagely repressed a wave of rage and nausea that swept through him at the man's impudence. Time, he told himself, there would be time to deal with him appropriately later. He gestured and the men, with uncertainty on their faces, brought themselves back to attention, turned in place, and marched back the way they'd come. It took them a long while, so indirect and lengthy was the route. All the while, Shanga leaned against his stony outcrop with a grin across his battered face.

"What have you got against Lando Calrissian, anyway, Gepta?"

The sorcerer's gaze jerked upward across the chamber to assure that no one else was present to witness the gibe. Then he settled back in his throne and stared coldly at the fighter pilot before him, struggling to maintain an even tone.

"It is sufficient that he has offended me—primarily with his impudence, Klyn Shanga, a fact you would do well to bear in mind. We have agreed upon the history of your woebegone system; tell me, what is *your* interest in a vagabond gambler. What has he to do with—"

In an instant, Shanga's façade of relaxation dropped away. He stood rigidly beside the stalagmite, his body trembling with anger. Rather a long time passed before he was able to reply.

"Calrissian doesn't figure in it. He has a partner—"

"The robot? Surely, Admiral—"

"*Robot!*" Shanga shot back hotly. "In the Renatasia it wasn't a robot, but a five-limbed organic sentient! I saw it then—nobody could avoid it! It was treated to parades and banquets, in the media every minute! It was an emissary from a long-lost galactic civilization that... that... that ultimately destroyed us! It was a spy, Gepta! It infiltrated us, observed our weaknesses, planned our downfall with ruthless precision! Robot? Oh yes, I saw it again after the battle of Oseon, disguised as a harmless droid, but I wasn't fooled, not for a nano! Robot? What would a robot have to gain from—"

Gepta raised an interrupting hand. He knew perfectly well why a droid might help destroy a system. Programmed to obey, it wouldn't have a choice, and properly disguised with an organic-appearing plastic coating, it would be a perfect spy. The sorcerer, however, wasn't about to argue with the man and possibly lose an ally. Shanga would have his uses—and his ultimate disposition.

"Very well, Admiral, we each of us have personal reasons for wishing a conclusion to this hunt, and your offer of assistance is welcome. But your communication hinted at more; there was a claim that you know where the *Millennium Falcon* may be found?"

"And *trapped*!" the warrior added with a snap in his voice. "Imagine the sweetness of it: trapped between us and the Centrality Navy!" He began laughing, the edge in his voice growing increasingly hysterical until he leaned heavily against the stone column, wiping his eyes and coughing. When he could speak again, it was only one word: "Starcave!"

Rokur Gepta kept his peace, offering no reply. The term was meaningless to him, but given an hour of privacy and access to his sources of information it would not remain so. Finally he replied. "Starcave, you say."

The fighter pilot nodded. "Yes, we have our spies among the Centrals, too, Gepta—we have to. After all, they're the ones who—but never mind that. The navy's keeping a heavy blockade there. We don't know why. There are rumors, but most of them are so silly that we think they're Centrality Intelligence cover. Whatever the reason, we also know that Calrissian's planning to run the blockade, in fact may be there as we speak. We have things you need: information, a rebuilt fighter squadron. You have something we need: passage through the blockade. With Calrissian bottled up there, we can..."

There was a very prolonged silence during which each of the figures savored his personal revenge. Gepta was secretly surprised that the Centrality military could mount a major action of that type without his knowing of it. On the other hand, he hadn't known about the Renatasian affair until years after it had happened. He was equally surprised at the depth—and enthusiasm—of Shanga's intelligence sources. After it was over, if he, the sorcerer, could incorporate...But that was for later. This was now, and the culmination of a very long, very annoying episode in the gray magician's otherwise unopposed rise to total power.

"Very well, Admiral Shanga, let us make an agreement between us. We shall go to this, this Starcave and see what may be seen. The refitting of the *Wennis* is nearly complete, and I will hurry the work. Your squadron will rendezvous with her at a place convenient to us both. I shall take us through the blockade, and you shall assist with the destruction of the *Millennium Falcon* and her owners. And afterward..."

Shanga stood, his right hand flexing where his blaster would have been hanging had it not been taken from him by Gepta's security people. He felt incomplete without it. There was a worn diagonal area across the lower half of his pressure suit, from high behind the left hip where the heavy belt ordinarily settled itself, to the middle of his right thigh where the weapon would have been strapped down.

"Yes," said the Admiral, "and afterward: what?"

The sorcerer smiled, an expression that manifested itself only in the sarcastic tone of his voice. Inside the dark gray windings about his hidden face, it was a far from pleasant expression.

"Afterward, my dear Admiral Shanga, we two shall go our separate ways, you to rebuild Renatasian civilization to glorious, dizzying new heights, while I, on the other hand—"

"Mynock muffins!" Shanga raised his gauntleted hand in a mocking salute. Then, without further ceremony, he turned on his space-booted heel and began the trek across the damp cavern floor to the elevator.

He itched to have his blaster once again—an itch he felt between his shoulder blades as he turned his back on the perfidious sorcerer—to get in his small fighter and rejoin the squadron hovering at the edge of the barren Tund System. The dead planet was giving him the creeps.

For his part, Gepta watched the figure of the Renatasian soldier diminish in the twilit distance, kneaded his gray-gloved hands together, once more stifling rage that bordered on gibbering insanity. To be walked out on by a mere underling! And especially one who possessed the gall to consider himself an equal partner in the sorcerer's affairs!

It was almost more than the ancient magician could bear. Almost.

There were rituals, however, formulae for calming both the mind and body under such nerve-shredding circumstances, venerable practices of the long-dead Sorcerers of Tund.

Rokur Gepta applied them all with a will.

FOUR

LANDO SAT IN THE COPILOT'S SEAT, SMOKING A CIGAR and thinking. The navy cruiser wasn't naked-eye visible and he had no desire to crank up the telescope. He'd seen a cruiser before.

They'd been given ten minutes to make up their minds: prepare for boarders or be obliterated. Lando was using every second of those minutes, trying to produce a third alternative. He wasn't having much luck. He'd known from the beginning that a moment like this was going to arrive, sooner or later—although he hadn't imagined it arriving quite so soon. The plans he'd sketched out in leisure and safety at their last port of call seemed fragile and silly now, however detailed and astute they had appeared at the time.

The trouble, of course, arose from the fact that Lehesu hadn't gone straight home. Fortune or coincidence hadn't had very much to do with his rescue. Lando and Vuffi Raa had stumbled across the same "desert" that had threatened to kill the young oswaft. What it meant for them and the *Falcon* was a sudden drop to below light-speed while Vuffi Raa recalibrated the engines. In the empty sector, the engines had met almost no resistance

and they threatened to race wildly until they tore themselves and their operators apart, atom by atom.

Thus they had been poking along on their reaction
drive when they'd encountered a five-hundred-meter
monster soaring from nowhere. At first they'd taken Lehesu for a weird ship from an unknown culture. They'd
been half right, but then Lehesu had mistaken the *Falcon*
for a being something like himself. It had taken much
longer to straighten out *that* misunderstanding than to
puzzle out the vacuum-breather's plight and do something
about it.

Vuffi Raa had, as usual, been at the controls, as Lando
kept a suspicious eye on Lehesu and a nervous thumb
on the trigger from the quad-gun blister.

*"Master, I have communications on a very unconven-
tional frequency."*

"What's being said?" Lando shifted the stump of his
cigar to the other side of his mouth, hunched over the
receiver of the quad-gun even farther, and strained to see
the weird object floating half a klick away. It was transparent, and didn't show up very well on the detectors,
as if it were made of plastic instead of metal. There was
no sign of shielding, and he'd seen much bigger ships.
Nevertheless, its casual proximity raised the fine hair on
the back of his neck and gave him the impulse to jam
the triggers down and keep them down until it was reduced to harmless vapor.

"I've got the Falcon's *computers working on it—they're
not very well suited to translation, I'm afraid—and I'm
also plugged into things myself. It would appear—wait!
We're starting to receive a visual array. Repeating that
first greeting seems to have done the . . . yes . . .
yes . . . Master! It's sending us a picture of ourselves!"*

♦ 29 ♦

Great, Lando thought, here we are, parsecs from any known civilization, and we've stumbled across an itinerant portrait photographer. Usually they brought a pony or a young Bantha with them, but . . . He let the sarcastic thoughts dribble away. They weren't doing any good. He trusted Vuffi Raa to handle things in general, but hated to put his life in *anybody's* hands but his own.

"Well, send them back a picture of themselves, for Core's sake! Pretend we're a pair of tourists taking each other's snapshots. It beats shooting it out."

"Yes, Master, I had already arrived at that conclusion, and am transmitting a slow-scan with the proper characteristics. I can put it on one of your gunnery screens if you think it's worth the risk."

"Go ahead. I can do better with the naked eye anyway, given our range and this thing's weird composition."

On a display to his left, the outline of the *Falcon*, as seen by the alien object, faded away to be replaced with an enhanced representation of the object itself. Vuffi Raa's vision was better than Lando's. He was making out or inferring a good deal more detail. The thing remarkably resembled some marine creatures Lando had seen in his travels although it was too large by at least an order of magnitude. It was also somewhat like a bird—

The picture jerked, the viewpoint changed, the object curled and uncurled its "wings."

"Master, this picture's coming from them! Master, I don't think this is a spaceship! I think it's a—"

At this point, Lehesu began his little video drama, showing himself starving to death and dying, then changing things to show himself feeding and prospering. By the time he was finished, Lando and Vuffi Raa had a much better idea of what they had encountered in that odd, empty region of interstellar space.

Lando knew that it was theoretically possible for or-

tages to having an electronic brain. What's he showing you, naked dancing-droids?"

"Master! *On the contrary, he's displaying things which he can fabricate from the chemicals he doesn't need in his food. Apparently he does it atom by atom. Master! He's showing me opals, sapphires, flame-gems and sunstones. Why, that's a life-crystal from the Rafa System! Lehesu, can you truly—"*

"Yes, my little friend, if these objects interest you. There is more, much more that I can make. But tell me, is it true that Master cannot see what I am showing you this moment, without an artifact to assist him?"

Lando interrupted. "Core blast you, Vuffi Raa, now you've got *him* calling me master! I want him to stop it immediately, do you hear me, Lehesu? And Vuffi Raa?"

"Yes, Master?"

"Come on inside and we'll take a look at what Lehesu's offering over a screen."

Lehesu's people, the oswaft, had had yet another talent, and that is what had gotten the young vacuum-breather into trouble, the second time.

The interior of the Starcave, over a dozen light-years in extent, was huge even for the relatively enormous organisms and the rest of the complex ecology that inhabited it. Simply boring along at sublight velocities, as Lehesu had been doing on his last (figurative) legs when the *Falcon* had found him, wasn't enough.

Lehesu hadn't gone straight home when he left the *Falcon*. His curiosity hadn't been satisfied—in fact it had been sharpened exponentially by contact with the human and the droid. He wanted to see what things were like in the regions of space that had produced them.

Holding firmly onto his canister of nutrients, he'd bidden them farewell and exchanged promises to get in touch again someday. The gambler had taken these no more seriously than any frequent traveler does with the strangers he gets to know superficially for a short time. He and Vuffi Raa had gone on about their own business, flipping switches and turning knobs to bring the *Falcon* up to full power once more when they reached the margin of the "desert."

Lehesu had gone in search of civilization.

Unfortunately for the oswaft and the subsequent security of his people, he had done his searching in a region patrolled by the Centrality navy, whose sensors, acquired at the unwilling expense of quadrillions of taxpayers, were more sophisticated than those of the *Falcon*. They'd ferreted out the truth about the strange being upon first spotting him, noticing an ability Lando and Vuffi Raa had missed: not only to soar through space in a linear fashion, but to "skip" vast distances when it suited him, as hyperdrive starships do. They'd tracked him back to the ThonBoka when he'd returned with joyous news of his discoveries.

The navy, of course, had recognized a threat when they saw one: a race of beings at home in space, capable of faster-than-light travel—a terrible thing to contemplate. Their scouts' estimate of the number of oswaft was even more terrifying. It was like encountering a previously unknown superpower with millions of fully operational starships. There was only one thing to do.

The ThonBoka was an open system. It had to be, or exhaust its resources rapidly. The idea was to starve the oswaft to death, denying them the chemicals drifting in on the galactic tide. Once the vacuum-breathers were sufficiently weakened, they could be finished off neatly, their threat erased forever.

But the Centrality Navy didn't know that Vuffi Raa's canister handiwork had included a radio relay and transducer—he had truly meant to stay in touch—through which Lehesu had shouted a cry for help across the parsecs. Lando, seeing in the creature's problems a solution to problems of his own, had loaded his ship and come arunning. Now he was having second thoughts.

Less than a hundred kilometers away, point-blank range as distances in space are reckoned, a Centrality battle cruiser waited impatiently for an answer. The *Falcon* was fast, but not fast enough to evade the vessel's tractor beams or destructive weaponry. As freighters go, she was well armed and heavily shielded against impecunious pirates and the usual run of free-lance riffraff one was likely to encounter in interstellar space. But her quadguns and other weaponry were no match for the armament sprouting from what seemed like every square meter of the warship that confronted them. And worse, at that range, the Falcon's shields would buy her only microseconds of extended life.

Lando considered running—not away from the nebula, but toward it—until he realized that a simple message from the picket vessel would have a hundred more just like it primed and ready by the time the *Falcon* got to the Starcave's mouth. He evaluated very carefully a slim number of other alternatives, compared them with his original plan, and shook his head. No two ways about it: the idea had been lousy to begin with, was still lousy, but it was the only one he had.

"Vuffi Raa," he said at last, closing his eyes as if that could shut out the images of disaster forming in his mind, "shut down all weapons systems as we discussed. Also power down the shields and make sure they can see what we've done over there on their scopes, will you?" He flipped a fifty-credit coin and caught it in the air.

Beside him, the robot sounded dubious. "But Master,

that will leave us completely helpless." His tentacles fidgeted on the control panels.

Lando grinned. "A long time ago, a machine of my acquaintance pointed out that a person who believes that violence is the first or only alternative is morally bankrupt." Up went the coin again, down into the gambler's palm, and up again.

Vuffi Raa stood silent. *He* had been the machine, and the occasion Lando's learning that the little droid was programmed against causing harm to any intelligent being.

"Right now, old can-opener," the gambler continued, "our mechanical defenses are a liability, the appearance of helplessness an asset. Long before I became a starship captain, I was a grifter and a hornswoggler. I guess it's time to see if I retain the skills." Lando walked the coin across the backs of his knuckles, and put it away.

The sound of chromium-plated metal tapping on plastic was loud as Vuffi Raa began the process of rendering the ship harmless. Lando sat, deep in thought, weighing his next words carefully.

At last: "All right, raise that cruiser out there; get them on the line. And cheer up—I know what I'm doing. I think."

The robot was incapable of facial expression, but his voice was ripe with worried skepticism. "What should I say, Master?"

Lando chuckled. "Don't call me master. Tell them we received their earlier messages, and that it's *they* who should be prepared to take on boarders!"

FIVE

Lando Calrissian had never particularly liked spacesuits.

Not only were they bulky and uncomfortable, they lacked elegance. His was maintained in the best condition possible, but the color combinations were egregious, the line was execrable, and it clashed with every formal and semiformal shipsuit he owned. And wrinkled them, as well.

Nevertheless, he was suited up and waiting by the topside lock as the *Falcon*, under Vuffi Raa's deft maneuvering, backed and filled to a designated place under the belly of the Centrality Cruiser *Respectable*. Beside him on the deckplates was a large soft-sided carrying case loaded with supplies and samples he'd purchased for just the occasion. It was one of those times when thorough preparation and a detailed plan instilled no confidence whatever.

"*Locking on, Master*," came the doubly electronic voice from the cockpit.

"All right, Vuffi Raa, don't wait up for me."

Lando gave the wheel above his head a full turn, another half turn, and cringed, as he always did, when it popped heavily out of its threads. He swung it to one side, reached down for his case, and made his clumsy way up the metal rungs of the ladder, through the *Falcon*'s hull, and into the receiving area aboard the *Respectable*.

To discover he was staring straight into the muzzles of half a dozen high-powered blasters.

Gulping—and happy that it was concealed by his helmet—Lando keyed his suit radio as he swung the heavy bag onto the deck of the cruiser, lifted himself up, and straightened.

"Good afternoon, gentlebeings. Lando Clarissian, interstellar trader at your service. What can I do you for?" He laughed heartily at his lame joke.

He'd climbed into a hangar bay. Lando thought it a little stupid that they hadn't been invited inside, freighter and all—the Centrals certainly had the room for it. The ceiling was invisible far above, drowned out by the harsh lights glaring down onto the deck. The chamber was at least two hundred meters from its broad, curving, and presently tightly shut doors to the complicated-looking rear wall where half a hundred windows lit in various colors showed control and maintenance areas behind a pressure bulkhead.

The squad of security guards didn't relax a millimeter. Their leader, identifiable by the insignia on his battle armor, crackled forward, slapped the weapon he was carrying across his chest.

"*Quiet, civilian! You are ordered to report, under arrest, to the sector security chief. Your baggage will be taken for inspection and decontamination!*"

"Decontamination?" Lando feigned dismay. "You want to decontaminate a dozen cartons of fine Dilnlexan cigars, Oseoni cigarettes, Trammistan chocolates—"

"*Cigars?*" the head goon asked in a rather different

tone of voice than before. He looked right and left, slapped a pair of switches on his arm panel, grabbed Lando's arm, and similarly rendered the gambler's suit radio inoperative. He touched his opaque-visored helmet to Lando's bubble.

"Cigars, you say? Do you know how long the Ship's Exchange has been out of cigars? We've been on picket at this Core-forsaken nebula since—*ahem*!" The man seemed to regain control of himself momentarily. "Report, with this escort, to the sector chief. I'll take custody of your sample case and make certain that its contents are undamaged."

"Although they may be somewhat depleted when I get them back?" Lando grinned and winked through two layers of plastic at the invisible face next to his. "Just keep in mind, Sergeant, that there's a lot more where this came from if we establish an amenable relationship, all right?"

The sergeant snapped to attention after switching on both radios again.

"Message received and understood, trader! I trust you'll enjoy your stay aboard the Respectable."

"Oh," Lando said, "I'm sure I will. Shall we be moving along?"

The sector chief was a grizzled, overweight warrant officer with hash marks on his uniform sleeves which threatened to dribble off his cuffs and onto the metal deckplates of his office. He scratched a crew-cut head and then shifted his hand to rub a bulbous, well-veined nose.

"Well, I ain't never heard of nothing like this before—a civilian merchant plyin' his wares to vessels on blockade duty. And friend, if I ain't heard of it before, you've got a problem, cause this man's navy operates on precedent."

Lando, having been examined, searched, scrutinized, peered at and into by human eyes and hands and the sensory ends of countless pieces of nastily suspicious equipment, leaned back in the chair across from the warrant officer's desk and nodded pleasantly. He was glad he'd selected his plainest, least colorful shipsuit to wear beneath his pressure outfit, which was hanging neatly in a locker near the hangar, and even gladder he'd left his tiny five-shot stingbeam aboard the *Falcon*. It was the only personal weapon he ordinarily allowed himself, but at the moment it would have been as conspicuous and counterproductive as his freighter's quad-guns.

"Believe me, Chief, I understand tradition. My family tree is full of it. But there ought to be room for a little enterprise and innovation, shouldn't there? As long as it doesn't jeopardize the mission, and is conducted through the proper channels?"

"Errhem!" The sector chief cleared his throat, inhaled from one of Lando's expensive cigars. The gambler's case lay on the floor beside his chair, as thoroughly inspected for weapons and instruments of sabotage as himself, and considerably lighter in weight than when he'd brought it aboard the cruiser. At each level of inspection, from the guard sergeant to the warrant officer, it had become slightly more empty, in proportion to the rank of the emptier.

"My precise sentiments, Chief. Now, about our arrangements. I suggest we route our marketing *around* the Ship's Exchange. In the first place, my overhead won't allow me to offer what I have at wholesale. In the second, I suspect buying from an itinerant peddler such as myself might provide an agreeable diversion for your troops. In the third—well, do you think there might be any interest aboard in games of chance?"

The warrant officer blinked. He fancied himself a sharp gambler and regarded all civilians everywhere as easy pickings, having spent decades taking things from them at large-bore gunpoint. He wasn't able to distinguish between this and situations where civilians had an even chance; could not, in fact, conceive of such circumstances.

"Games of chance? Such as?..."

"Such as *sabacc*." Lando smiled. "I'm something of an enthusiast, and it would offer you and yours a small opportunity to get your money back for whatever you happen to buy—'you' being a figurative expression in this instance, on account of your commission."

"Commission?" The sector chief looked confusedly at the stripes on his sleeve, then suddenly at the cigar he was smoking. "Oh, *commission*! I get it! Actually, it's a warrant. But no matter! Very funny!"

Lando hadn't intended it to be, but he laughed heartily along until the creature subsided. Then the sector chief adopted an expression that he imagined was shrewd, having practiced it before a mirror since he was a rating.

"I'm sure a few games might be arranged, for a suitable *commission*!" He broke into guffaws again, and Lando stifled a self-destructive urge to strangle the uniformed baboon with his own hash marks.

"Very well. Now there's one more thing I'd like to ask about. I hesitate, because I have some idea of the importance of your mission here—"

"*You do?*" The chief surged forward, leaning avidly across his desk. Only the artificial gravity of the floorplates kept him planted on his swivel chair.

A wave of alarm swept through the gambler's body. He'd said the wrong thing. This mission was supposed to be top secret, and, furthermore, was an unusually shameful one, even for the Centrality navy. His mind raced, trying to find a way to salvage something from the mess his careless tongue had created.

"Tell me," the chief said before Lando could speak. "It's the ranks that always know the least, and the folks back home who have a better picture of what's going on." He peered about the room, rose, slid a picture of the fleet commodore aside, seized a small plastic bulb hanging from a wire behind the picture, and closed his hand around it, covering it completely.

"Bugs," the chief said. "We can speak freely now. What *is* so important about this mission?"

Lando almost wept with relief. Then he had to do some fast thinking. "I've heard they have more pirate ships bottled up inside that nebula than have ever been seen in one place before. Apparently Intelligence tricked them into some kind of rendezvous, and you're keeping them trapped until they can be destroyed."

The chief nodded sagely. "That makes some sense of the scuttlebutt I've heard. Any idea when we're going in?"

Lando shook his head. "You know the navy: 'hurry up and wait.'"

Again the knowing, comradely nod. Lando had a friend, now; he revised his prices upward 20 percent. "Sounds like you were maybe a navy man yourself," the chief suggested.

Lando returned the nod. "Just a swabbie, when I was a kid," he lied. "Never made it big, like you, Chief."

"Well, we all have our place in the scheme of things, son. They also serve who only—"

"Sell cigars? And while we're speaking of cigars, why don't you have half a dozen of these for later, Chief. A man only gets so many luxuries, out here on the front line."

"*Sabacc!*" the excited rating cried, gathering in a pot that wouldn't have paid for one of Lando's cigars. The gambler made a practice of losing loudly on the small bets and raking in the winnings as inconspicuously as possible when the stakes were high. Now he was following a policy of steady losses on nearly every hand, in order to win the larger game that awaited him in the ThonBoka.

It was the fourth cruiser he and Vuffi Raa had visited in as many days, using the original warrant officer's connections. Each transfer, ship-to-ship, with its attendant docking and security procedures growing laxer and more perfunctory, brought the *Millennium Falcon* and her real cargo closer to the Starcave and its waiting denizens.

The freighter hadn't been immune to searches, but nobody wastes much time—or olfactory sensibilities—on the trash and toilet recyclers, especially when they were genuinely full of substances that everyone heartily regarded as filth. And especially when no one below the rank of admiral seemed to know the reason behind the stupid blockade.

Lando was rapidly coming to love military security procedures.

With inexpert hands made clumsier by petty greed, the rating dealt the cards out. There were seventy-eight of them, divided into five suits: Sabres, Staves, Flasks, and Coins, arrayed from Aces to Masters, and a special suit of face cards with negative values and more profound meanings. The object of the game was simplicity itself: acquire cards until the value of your hand was exactly twenty-three, or as close as you could get without going over. A perfect zero or a minus twenty-three was as bad as a twenty-four, and there were certain special hands, such as that combining a Two of anything, a Three of anything, and an Idiot from the special suit, which ritual decreed were the equivalent of twenty-three.

The game being played in the cruiser *Reliable*'s MessRec area included Lando, two cooks, and a pair of low-ranking gunners. Lando wore his most tattered clothing, pressed with razor creases, for the occasion.

What made *sabacc* really interesting—and destroyed the nerves of most amateurs who tried to play it—was that each card was an electronic chip, capable of changing face and value at random any moment until the card-chip was lying flat on a gaming table or upon the electronic mat Lando had provided. Thus a winning hand, held too long, could change spontaneously to garbage, or, more rarely, a mess of meaningless numbers could become a palladium mine.

Lando found the game relaxing and a welcome change from the exigencies of interstellar freight-hauling. He'd always enjoyed it, no matter the stakes, possibly because he found it quite difficult to lose. Even honestly.

The older of the two cooks took the hand and the deal shifted to him accordingly. He'd won perhaps half what the previous winner had and was looking inordinately pleased with himself. Lando inwardly shook his head, remembering times when the ransom for a princess or the price of a starship had rested before him on a table in the most exclusive and luxurious settings imaginable. It was difficult to keep the right perspective, to remember from moment to moment that the real stakes here were the highest he'd ever played for: the survival of an entire race, and whatever he might demand in fabricated precious stones indistinguishable from nature's best.

With pitiable awkwardness, the cook dealt Lando a

pair of card-chips from the bottom of the deck, attempting to cheat the others in the process as well. Not only wasn't he good at it, he wasn't *any* good at it. Lando received a Master of Staves, worth fourteen points, and a Nine of Flasks: a natural two-card twenty-three. The gambler held them back, hoping one or the other would metamorphose into something worthless. He wasn't after the pay of those miserable sailors, but information.

"Well," he said casually, "I've almost sold my quota here on the *Reliable*. You swabbies have any suggestions where I might find greener pastures?"

His connections, compliments of the *Respectable*'s sector chief, had about run dry, and he needed not only the name of the next ship closer to the mouth of ThonBoka, but of someone aboard in a position to do him some good. As bets were placed and extra cards were passed around; Lando asked for one, giving up the Commander. He received an Ace of Coins just as the Nine in his hand transformed itself into an Eight—*another* pestiferous twenty-three!

All right, then: "*Sabacc!*" the gambler said for the first time that afternoon. You lose some, you win some; you gotta take the good with the bad. He raked in a few millicredits and promptly engineered a loss again. It was simpler to do when he had control of the cards.

"You might try the *Courteous*," the younger of the two cooks suggested, pushing his white hat back from his sweaty forehead. He smelled of onions and had a missing tooth. "Those boys been on the line longer'n anybody here. I got a cousin-in-law over there who says— *OW!*"

"Oh he does, does he?" observed Lando, watching the older cook kick the younger under the table. "Accident-prone or just sensitive to pain?"

♦ 45 ♦

"You gotta keep your flapping lip buttoned, Merle," the older cook said, "There's sucha thing as security."

"Aww, Clive, Lando's all right. Usta be a rating hisself, didn't you, Lando? He just wants to sell stuff over on the *Courteous*, like he done here, ain't that right, Lando? An' seein' as it's the closest ship in, he might be able to get a look at what the fuss is—*OW!*"

The older cook looked apologetic. "No offense, Mr. Calrissian."

Lando grinned as he watched the younger cook rub a tender shin. "None taken."

It was a cheerful tune the young gambler was whistling as he shinnied down the ladder into the airlock of the *Millennium Falcon*. "Honey, I'm home!"

"Are you referring to me, Master?" Vuffi Raa asked, maneuvering his tentacles over the hatchway coaming. He took Lando's helmet, helped his master raise the circular overhead hatch and screw it into place.

"Did you take care of that little job I asked you about?" the gambler inquired. They passed along the corridor to the cockpit. Lando stopped to inspect his quad-guns. The fleet security force's seals were still in place; the weapons were theoretically inoperable. Vuffi Raa had cheated around them the first hour they'd been installed.

"Why yes, Master, I have. Can you tell me now why you wanted such an odd thing done?" Strapping himself into place, the robot received clearance from the *Respectable* and detached the *Falcon* from her belly.

Lando glanced suspiciously around the cabin. "You tell me: can I let you in on it without informing the boys in gray up there?"

The little droid sounded a bit scandalized. "Master, I removed a total of twenty-three listening devices from this vessel, put there by at least three separate agencies in the last seventy-one hours. We're completely clean. What I'd like to know is why you wanted—"

"Simple. I want you to raise the *Courteous*, confirm we're on our way, and set a course for her. Then I want you to be ready to punch everything we've got into the drives, and everything else into the aft shield-generators, as soon as we pass by her and light out for the ThonBoka. Got that?" He reached under the control panel, extracted a cigar of a quality much higher than the ones he had been selling. Vuffi Raa lit it for him with a tentacle tip.

"Aye, aye, Master. But that device you had me construct while you were aboard the *Respectable*: it projects at least a meter beyond the after shields, and it's—"

"*Courteous*, this is *Millennium Falcon* if you're reading. As per previous permission, we're on our way over. I've got a hundred gallons of beebleberry ice cream I've been saving especially for you. Over."

"But Master, we don't have any—"

"Em Falcon, *this is* Courteous. *We haven't had any kind of ice cream aboard for weeks. You're highly welcome, and we hear you have in interest in statistics.*"

Lando laughed at the universal gambler's code. "Permutations and combinations of the number seventy-eight, *Courteous*—fives are wild. Watch for us at your airlock any minute now. Out."

The *Falcon* soared under reaction drive across the distance between the two warships, Lando worrying every moment that his idea and the device he'd had Vuffi Raa construct would actually work. It was the most terrible risk he'd ever taken, with no time to experiment, and technologics were not exactly his bailiwick. If it failed, then they'd be little metal splinters scattered from there to the Rafa System.

"Millennium Falcon, *you're off the beacon! Where'd you learn to fly that overstuffed horseshoe, you con-*

founded feather merchant, some charm school some-where?"

Critical moments ticked by, during which the *Falcon* refrained from replying to the innuendo—and precious kilometers toward her goal racked themselves up on the boards.

"Em Falcon, *now hear this! Correct course immediately! Our guns are bearing on you, do you copy?"*

Gritting his teeth and clamping nervous hands securely over the arms of his chair, Lando sat motionless, watching the dials. A trickle of sweat ran down the side of his neck into his collar, but he said nothing.

Once more: "Millennium Eff, *you've got five seconds from the mark, and then you'll be nothing but incandescent atoms! Mark: five, four, three . . ."*

"Okay, Vuffi, this is it! As soon as the drives are hot, punch everything she's got!"

"Very well, Master."

The robot's tentacles were a confusing blur over the ship's control console as he diverted power to the after shields until the gauges screamed at the incipient overload. Lights began twinkling cheeringly across the section of the panels labeled FTL; the powerful interstellar drives awoke from several days' unwilling somnolence. Finally, all boards were green. Drives and shields were ready as the navy voice in the com reached zero.

Lando hoped his invention was ready, too.

"Millennium Falcon," the communicator warned a final, unnecessary time—giving the gambler and the droid an extra few seconds—"*you're a dead—"*

"*Now!"* Lando and Vuffi Raa screamed at the same time.

The voice chopped off. The after shields blossomed into an invisible protective canopy while the ultralight-speed generators began to throb—just as the leading wave front of the first meter-thick destructor beam from the cruiser struck the *Falcon* squarely in the center of her stern.

Her shields held . . . and held . . . and—

Suddenly the *Millennium Falcon* burst into an enormous blinding cloud of rapidly dispersing gases; a rain of metallic particles glittered, occupying the space where she had been.

SIX

THE ONE ADDRESSED THE OTHER: "AT LONG LAST, IT is nearly time."

Like Lehesu of the oswaft, he swam comfortably in emptiness, absently contemplating the surrounding stars. Unlike Lehesu, he knew everything about them, had been to visit many of them himself. Nor was that the only way that he was not like the ThonBoka vacuum-breather. Even Lando Calrissian, accustomed to many strange and wonderful sights, would have had trouble recognizing the entity as a living being.

"Yes," the Other replied, although his companion's statement had been rhetorical. "All things are now as they have been planned. I shall gather the Rest, and they shall accompany us."

He took action to accomplish just that. Such were the distances involved that, even at communications speeds exponential to that of light, it would require several days to achieve the desired transfer of information.

"Indeed," the One agreed. "That, too, is as it has been planned. It is very strange, my friend, this 'not-knowing,' stranger than I had anticipated. Quite an uncomfortable feeling, really. It has been so long since . . ." He let what served him for a voice trail off, contemplating a gulf of time the mere thought of which might have driven a lesser being to gibbering disconnection.

The Other indicated silent sympathy. He, too, had experienced the discomfort of uncertainty, and, despite his almost unimaginable life-span, and the relatively recent character of the events, for far too long. Uncertainty was like that. However, that had been the very purpose of the plan. Over the countless eons of their existence, the One, the Other, and the Rest had become, in a manner of speaking, too perfect, too well-informed. It had become all too easy to anticipate events simply from long experience with reality, excellent sources of information, and well-practiced logic.

Ironically, it was in that manner that the One had originally foreseen racial stagnation and eventual death did these comfortable circumstances continue. He had advised all concerned that an element of the unknown be reintroduced. They, of course, had seen the sense of it and agreed (with a cordiality that was itself symptomatic; a more vital, lusty people would have included a number of individuals who were contrary just for the sake of contrariness.) Their first experiment in guesswork, partial knowledge, and risk was maturing now, a process some thousands of years in the making.

"Do you suppose . . ." the Other began, unconsciously reviving a long-unused turn of phrase as he let the unproductive thought trickle away. At that point speculation was futile. He knew as well as the One what consequences, in all their manifest likelihoods, were possible, from a vast unprecedented enrichment of their ancient, already lavishly complex culture, to its uttermost destruction. These were not beings to whom such gambling came easily or naturally—which was yet another reason why it had become necessary. "Do you suppose? . . ."

The One replied, "I do not know—How truly unsubstantial a sensation! For the first time in eons we shall learn New Things, regardless of the outcome. These we shall have to integrate with the old, producing syntheses unlooked for. I feel . . . this emotion must be very much as our ancestors experienced when scarcely anything was known, and everything remained yet to be learned. It is little wonder they were half mad and came close, times without number, to destroying themselves."

After a long period of silence, the Other said, "I have learned a New Thing already." In the tone of his voice there was an odd, semiforgotten, yet somehow familiar difference.

But excitement tinged the voice of the One: "Please tell me—what is it? I, too, must learn this New Thing, and we must pass it on to—"

"I have learned that the prospect of learning New Things makes you unreasonably loquacious. I am not certain—there it is again, that 'not knowing'—that this is altogether good."

"I believe," the One replied rather stiffly, "that you have reinvented humor. And I am not certain whether that is good."

Klyn Shanga raced through endless night to join his makeshift squadron. Considering his three careers—soldier for his nation-state, farmer upon military retirement, soldier again for a hastily united and inevitably defeated Renatasian System—this last, the seeking of ultimate vengeance, was quite the strangest.

Shanga leaned back in his patched and shabby acceleration couch, carefully placing his feet between control pedals, stretching his long legs and arching his back to relieve an aching stiffness born more, on this occasion, of emotional tension than of lengthy travel. He was well practiced at that, having logged an incredible number of intersystem parsecs in his unlikely machine.

His blaster, its grips polished smooth by use, its muzzle bright with holster-wear and pitted by many more firings than it had been designed for, once again clung comfortingly to his thigh. It was not that having the weapon made him a whole man; like most professional soldiers, he was revolted by killing and avoided it whenever he could. Besides, he could do more damage to an opponent with his left elbow than most individuals could with an entire arsenal. But, like the battered, ancient ship he flew, it was an accustomed extension of his body, a companion and friend.

He had very few others left.

Somewhere ahead, hovering at the deep-frozen margin of the Tund System, his tiny fleet awaited the news he carried. They had towed themselves originally into this sector of the galaxy—a long, long way from home—by means of a scrapped and resurrected Centrality battleship engine that had been left among the ruins of their civilization by the departing marauders. To this they had attached, by cable, craft bought, stolen, and traded from a hundred cultures. Ultimately, the engine had become a weapon of despair, a fusion-powered battering ram. Even so, they had failed to accomplish their purpose for it, the destruction of Vuffi Raa.

Now, deprived of an independent method of ultralightspeed travel, they had to rely upon an uncertain ally. One who, without question, would betray them in the end.

Alone in the cramped cockpit of his fighter, Shanga reviewed the words he would employ to persuade his men that he had made the best of a bad bargain—those few who had survived the voyage to the Tund System and their first bloody encounter with the enemy at the Oseon. More had joined them afterward, dribbling out in the filthy holds of ancient freighters, hitching rides aboard the interstellar garbage scows.

Ironically, it was Rokur Gepta who, more than anybody else, represented the malign spirit that had destroyed the Renatasia. Somehow, too, it was fitting that they plotted together to use the navy as a sort of backstop against which they could crush their common foes. That same Centrality navy had been the direct agent of the home system's destruction. At the beginning of his vindictive adventure, Klyn Shanga had been fatalistically resigned to throwing away his life and the lives of his threadbare commands in order to avenge their titanic losses. Now he realized with increasing clarity and weariness that there was more—much more—to live for. The capture and slow termination of the five-legged infiltrator would only begin the process. Somehow they must make their mark upon the navy, upon the Centrality itself, upon everyone responsible in any way for the murder of a civilization.

Hopelessness breeds desperate measures. A partnership with the Sorcerer of Tund necessarily included a risk that the pitiable remains of Renatasian manhood might be used to some surpassingly evil purpose, to fulfill some objective even more hideous than the obliteration of a system-wide culture. If anyone was capable of engineering such a cataclysm, it was Rokur Gepta.

There was a Renatasian animal that planted itself by the waterside and, in the process of giving birth, provided fodder for a predacious toothy swimmer. Gepta was very much like that toothy swimmer, circling expectantly.

Shanga, with his tiny fleet (call it, rather, a "school") felt very much like that hapless littoral creature who must die herself—sacrificing, as well, a certain percentage of her young—in order to give whatever microscopic meaning to life that it was capable of possessing.

On the other hand, only sentient beings were foolish enough to imagine that the universe was anything but a sadistic battlefield where brutality was the natural order and agonized screaming provided the background music. Not even a man as bitterly demoralized as Klyn Shanga believed there was any meaning to death.

Perhaps he should never have retired from the military, he thought with a deeply felt sigh uncharacteristic of the role he presently played or the place he found himself now. All those years on his farm, amid fresh, growing things under a kindly sky, had made him far too philosophical to be a good soldier ever again. But he was all his world had left, so he would have to do.

Klyn Shanga flew onward through the star-strewn darkness, reviewing the words he would employ to persuade his men. He wished fervently they were of some use persuading himself.

Rokur Gepta, traveling aboard the refitted cruiser *Wennis*, was receiving an alarming report from one of his advance escorts. The flyer had returned in a one-seat fighter approximating the size and combat capabilities of Klyn Shanga's, but which was equipped—and this was rare, even for the Centrality navy—to exceed the speed of light. The little ship was half engine, virtually unarmed, and a tight fit, even for a slender youth. Piloting such a vehicle for more than a few minutes brought new meaning to the word "discomfort."

It and its occupant had been to the ThonBoka and back again already while the lumbering *Wennis*, considered a very sprightly vessel for its class, was still many days' journey from the nebula.

Gepta had such a fighter for his personal use. It had saved his life at least twice. He came as close to feeling fond of it as he came to feeling fond of anything—aside from the grim denizens from the darker recesses of his cavern on Tund. Fondness was not an emotion ordinarily to be discovered within the similarly stygian depths of Rokur Gepta's soul, although whether it had never lived within him, or had been ruthlessly exterminated early in his life, was a question that perhaps even the sorcerer was not prepared to answer.

Thus it was with something of a shock, in the brief instant before he regained control of himself, that Gepta experienced an unfamiliar, transient, and microscopic pang of personal regret as he learned of the destruction of the *Millennium Falcon* and her crew by the blockade cruiser. While the sorcerer wasn't watching, Lando Calrissian had somehow risen unbidden from the ranks of petty annoyance to that of worthy opponent and honored enemy.

"I saw it myself, sir!" the breathless scout gasped as moisture from the surrounding air condensed upon his space-cold armor and trickled off into a little pool on the deck plates. Like those of all his comrades attached to the mysterious *Wennis*, his Centrality gray uniform was unadorned by signs of rank or unit in order to preserve certain political fictions which his masters cherished. That no creature wiser than a sponge was taken in by such an exercise constituted no good reason not to pursue it.

Likewise, the slowly warming pressure suit he wore over his uniform, having just a few moments before leaped out of his cramped, ultrafast spacecraft into the cavernous hangar deck of the supposedly civilian cruiser, was without markings. Most of the personnel aboard the *Wennis*, being professional soldiers, resented the shallow deception, but, with understandable circumspection, seldom got around to mentioning it aloud.

While in command of the *Wennis*, Rokur Gepta did not affect the basaltic throne and the splendid isolation he preferred on Tund. He occupied the captain's acceleration chair (although there was an officer on board who claimed the title) and supervised his underlings on the bridge as they manipulated the controls at his bidding. He pitilessly examined the incoming scout, wondering whether, after all the time, all the effort, someone else had casually robbed him of victory over his prey.

"What ship, again?" the sorcerer hissed, briefly contemplating punishing its captain and crew. "Which ship destroyed the *Millennium Falcon*, and by what means?" The sorcerer hunched over like a scavenger bird, peering through the windings of his headdress, his eyes a pair of glowing, pulsating coals.

The rest of the bridge crew paid close attention to their consoles, cringing at the pilot's plight, but unwilling to interfere with his presumed destiny. They had seen a captain stripped of dignity and killed in that very place. They held out little hope for a mere lieutenant.

The scout gulped visibly, wishing he was back inside the claustrophobic confines of his craft. He was the best pilot aboard the *Wennis*, possibly one of the best in Centrality service. That was not going to do him any good with the sorcerer. Nor had he been educated to say or do the diplomatic thing when confronted with malevolent and arbitrary authority, at least of such potency. He felt he would have been better served had such a skill been part of his otherwise exhaustive military survival training—seldom had the need arisen for making a fire with flint and steel or using a signal mirror to summon help.

"The *Courteous*, sir," he answered finally, "part of the blockade line at the ThonBoka. In fact, sir, at the time, she was the closest vessel to the nebula. I listened to the traffic, sir, as I had been about to report aboard the flagship on your orders, and was awaiting docking clearance. This *Em Falcon*, an ugly old tub of a tramp freighter, was supposed to rendezvous with *Courteous* for purposes of trade. She'd been through the whole fleet that way, peddling tobacco and other civilian stuff like a vendor droid at a ballgame. Instead, she attempted to evade the cruiser and made high speed for the mouth of the nebula. That's when *Courteous* caught her. I never saw a beam like that before, sir. Must be something new."

Gepta leaned forward even farther, towering from his pedestaled chair over the young officer. "And the *Millennium Falcon*? What of her?"

The pilot gulped again, appreciating well the fate of innocent bearers of bad tidings. "Vaporized, sir. She took the full force on her after shields and overloaded. It was visible all over the fleet. Sir."

"So . . ." The sorcerer considered these data, the scout virtually forgotten as the young man stood before him, trembling at attention, his helmet under his arm. A runnel of sweat slowly crept down the side of the pilot's neck into the metal pressure collar of his suit.

The gray-swathed sorcerer glanced up again a moment later, almost absently. "Are you still here, Lieutenant? I suggest you report back to your section immediately."

The room fairly creaked with sudden relaxation.

An astonished and highly relieved young courier saluted his commander gratefully and departed the bridge amid the silent cheers of the cruiser's conspicuously disinterested crew members.

Looking forward to a good meal and something tall and cool to drink in the pilot's lounge below, the lieutenant passed through the bulkhead doors with a new spring in his step. The panels whispered closed behind him as he stepped into the companionway.

A large security trooper, one of Gepta's personal bodyguards, came up behind him, laid a hand the size of a telecom directory on the young man's shoulder. The lieutenant nearly jumped out of his spacesuit.

"Thought you'd bought the farm there, didn't you, son?" The older man's face crinkled in a grin that was difficult to interpret. "Say, I'm just going off duty, and seeing as how I was aboard the first time we ran into that garbage scow the *Falcon*, and seeing as how *I'm* just as pleased she's a cloud of radioactive dust, what do you say we both go below for some liquid celebration?"

The lieutenant looked up uncertainly into the trooper's face. The clamplike grip on his shoulder gave him little choice. He nodded without enthusiasm, and the two dwindled and disappeared down the corridor.

A short time later, Rokur Gepta stirred from futile contemplation, held up a gloved hand, and snapped his fingers.

From somewhere aft and overhead there came a rustle of dry, hairy wings as one of his pets lurched out of its darkened, foul-smelling niche, flapped across the room trailing an indeterminate number of scrawny, many-jointed legs. It came to rest, perching blindly on Gepta's outstretched wrist, salivating in anticipation just as the bodyguard entered the bridge with a small, shallow tray.

With his free hand, Gepta accepted a pair of plastic

tongs, reached for something on the tray, and held it up before his pet. The creature had nothing resembling a face, simply a gummy puckered opening toward the front of its body, set between the wings. The cavity distended greedily at the touch of the offered morsel.

There was a moment of enjoyment, some sucking, digestive noises. . . . It belched.

SEVEN

LEHESU CAME AS CLOSE TO NERVOUS PACING AS ANY oswaft could.

The giant raylike creature drifted in the relative emptiness of space at what he regarded a prudent distance from the warship-guarded mouth of the ThonBoka.

Watching the watchers.

As always, his estimate of what was prudent differed somewhat from that of his cosapients. None of them could be persuaded to venture within light-years of the spot from which the periodic activities of their new enemies could be observed, if not entirely understood. Restless, Lehesu concentrated a moment, got his bearings in some manner no one but another oswaft would be able to fathom, and *hopped*, without thinking much more about it, a few hundred thousand kilometers, as if the intervening distance didn't exist. It was a gesture of frustration. He had been brought up to believe such fidgeting was infantile, undignified, not to mention impolite when in the company of others. But at the moment he couldn't help himself. He was impatient, an emotion he shared in common with other species, but which would be beyond the comprehension of most oswaft. Still he waited.

He wasn't at all certain when Lando, Vuffi Raa, and the *Falcon* would arrive. He had difficulty yet, realizing that the freighter was not a real person. The existence of, and his friendship with, the chromium-plated robot made this realization even more difficult to achieve. That they would not fail to come to his aid he never doubted for an instant, despite the genteel jeering of family and friends. They had not believed the least of his tales about the Open Sea until the evidence had thundered up to the ThonBoka mouth, heavily gunned and, for some reason, angrily disposed toward the vacuum-breathing race.

This, of course, was somehow the adventuring Lehesu's fault.

Concerning Lando Calrissian . . . The oswaft's brief sojourn into human territory still hadn't educated him about cats; however there were certain aspects of that animal's psychology he might have identified with. Hadn't the gambler and his friends saved his life? Twice?

They were obligated, now.

Anxiety shifted Lehesu again, this time a quarter of a light-year, to one side of the nebula mouth, before he fully noticed it. He could "see" better from that vantage anyway. Metallic motes lost against a starry backdrop, the elements of the Centrality fleet themselves were invisible at this distance. But the aggregate was *noisy*. A welter of communication darted from ship to ship in a complex net of energies the operators of which fondly imagined was private. Lehesu had learned Lando's language in a matter of hours. It did not occur to him that the stirrings and mixings of ideas that constituted top-secret military codes were anything other than amusing games to those who employed them. He puzzled them out in idle moments, much faster than he'd overcome the initial difficulty presented by communicating with the gambler and the robot.

Had those in command of the fleet, those who had ordered its destructive presence outside the ThonBoka, become aware of that minor oswaft capability, they would have redoubled their efforts to exterminate the space people. In this instance, ignorance was mutual; Lehesu hadn't a notion of the threat he and his people represented to those who cherished power for its own sake.

A small, thin cloudlet of interstellar plankton drifted by, borne on the complex tide of gravity and photon pressure, tiny pseudoanimals and quasi-plants that formed the basis of the oswaft diet, indeed for the diet of all the thousands of space-evolved species living in the shelter of the Starcave. Lehesu nibbled at them in a desultory fashion. To the small extent he was aware of them, he realized they didn't taste particularly good. There was a reason for that: they were slowly dying.

The bottom rung of the ThonBoka food ladder was being ruthlessly and deliberately sawed out from under the rest of the nebula's ecology. Every now and again the vessels of the picket fleet outside would blossom into glowing visibility as, in concert, they unleashed titanic energies, saturating the space around themselves with destructive particles and waves. It was at these moments that Lehesu (who had found it necessary to explain to his people something he didn't altogether understand himself: that these were not living organisms that beseiged them, but artifacts *containing* living organisms) could see that the blockading fleet formed a carefully calculated pattern through whose fields of fire not one molecule of preorganic substance could sift unassaulted.

What did come through was spoiled and tasted terrible.

If that were not enough, the ships sprayed a kind of poison—enzymes designed to smash the complex natural molecular arrangements of deep space, reduce them to constituent atoms, and destroy their nutritive value. The oswaft and their environment were being coldly and systematically starved to death by an implacable enemy they did not know, hadn't picked, had owed no animosity.

Until now.

"Yellow Niner, this is Hosrel XI Perimeter Control, we have a bandit at coordinates three-five-oh-two-three. Do you copy? Over."

The young rating at the sensor screen had been bored until then. She had been bored for thirty-four solid weeks, and the constant drills, the frontier-duty pay, the promise of a chance at a commission, hadn't helped. Not a bit. But she was no longer bored. If the bogey was a drill, it was something new. At that top-secret navy base on the freeze-dried edge of an already unspectacular system, *anything* new, however potentially threatening to life, limb, or the continued wearing of a gray Centrality uniform, was highly welcome.

"*Perimeter Control*," the interceptor pilot replied with a studied drawling casualness that belied the fact that he was a year younger than the sensor operator, "*we copy. This is Yellow Nine Leader. Are you requesting a six-sixty-six? Over?*"

The operator leafed quickly through her procedures manual. It was so hard remembering . . . yes, there it was: six-sixty-six, scramble and visual checkout of an unidentified target. Scrambling, in effect, was already taken care of: Hosrel XI Command kept at least one full interceptor squadron spaceborne on the perimeter all the time, and Yellow Niner was *it*, at the moment. She hadn't any idea what was being defended at the Core-forsaken base. Probably the navy was developing something unimportant, but they were giving security all the ruffles and flourishes.

"Yellow Niner, that's affirmative. Give me your ETVC. Over."

"My what? Oh yeah: we ought to be eyeballing your bogey in about, oh, call it seven minutes, give or take. Got it on the scope repeater, now. Looks kinda like it's made of plastic, doesn't it? Over."

Both the interceptor pilot and the sensor operator had been briefed, fairly recently, on new developments in camouflaging shields. But neither could discuss it in the clear over an open communications band. Security is a sword that cuts both ways, and most often wounds the hand that wields it.

"Yes, yes it does, Yellow Niner. I have your ETVC at six minutes, now. Is that about right? Over."

"Yeah, yeah. Yellow Nine Squadron, this is Yellow Nine Leader. As far as I know, this is no drill, repeat, no drill. Unlock your arming switches and keep the thumb you aren't sitting on near the button. No mistakes, now, or we'll all be plucking crystals in the life-orchards. Out to you, and over to PC."

PC, thought the Operator, that sounded sort of nice and heroically terse. She said nothing, but simply watched a dozen hard, sharp, shiny blips converge on the single fuzzy, almost invisible one. She had already sent nervous fingers flying over an alphanumeric pad, alerting her superiors to the situation, and other eyes were monitoring other scopes, now, within the subterranean bowels of the installation. She fastened her military collar and straightened a crease. Almost, she hoped, the target would be a genuine pirate attack or rebel uprising. Promotions came fast in times of—

"Perimeter Control, this is Yellow Nine Leader. Where the Core is this thing? We oughta be right on top of it, unless you're—by the Great Lens, there it is! It's huge

and clear as glass! We're making our first pass, using prerecorded hailing signals ...oh yeah: over."

The strange vessel failed to respond, at least on frequencies the interceptors were permitted to receive. Instead, it simply disappeared as the squadron crowded it, leaving the fighters to mill around an empty spot like moths around a light that is suddenly turned out.

It reappeared to one side, a few thousand meters away, just as Yellow Nine Seven passed beneath its transparent wing, which twitched involuntarily as Lehesu struggled to regain his balance. Suddenly Yellow Nine Seven corkscrewed away, a smoking, flaming ball of crumpled metal, its pilot screaming something into his helmet mike about his deflector shields having failed to function properly.

The voice bit off suddenly.

Eleven pilots whipped their ships around savagely. Eleven thumbs mashed down upon their firing studs. Twenty-two eyes widened as eight destructive beams—three had not been maintenanced correctly—converged on empty space. One interceptor, Yellow Nine Four, was caught in the crossfire. He'd failed to make a turn, due to faulty attitude-control, and vanished in a flash of energy and atomized debris.

Lehesu stepped off half a light-year, astounded at the hostile reaction he'd encountered, not at all like his first contact with the *Millennium Falcon*. And his people thought *he* was crazy. With the oswaft equivalent of a shrug, he turned his face toward yet another star whose spectrum showed traces of artificial, highly ordered radiation, and prepared himself for a longer jump this time.

Unaware that a densely cloaked scout vessel was right behind him.

The next system had been much the same, except ...
They'd been forewarned, somehow, of this bizarre

unidentified craft that had managed to destroy three (Yellow Nine Nine had missed the mouth of its Launch/Reentry tunnel and splashed itself all over a mountainside of frozen nitrogen; little squiggles of liquid helium danced with glee at the sight) first-rate Centrality fighter-interceptors. The new group also ignored his frantic, placative signaling and suffered forty-three casualties, some of them on the ground, due to an unfortunate change of shift going on between two double-strength squadrons. Lehesu had given up and gone home.

Eventually the fleet had made its appearance. The ordeal was a little more bearable for Lehesu than for the others. He was the only oswaft in a hundred generations who had come close to dying by starvation once before. As some human philosopher in a different time and place would observe, that which fails to kill us strengthens us. Lehesu knew his limits; he could tell that the pogrom was going to take rather a longer time than either side realized. To his less adventurous comrades, it was already agony, already an unprecedented emergency. They felt, for the first time in their long, long lives, a relatively mild discomfort, and were afraid. Some actually spoke of attempts to negotiate, to establish upon what terms the Centrals would let them live, not knowing that their utter destruction was the only success the fleet's mission profile recognized.

Lehesu wished his people would get angry, instead.

Thus, he waited.

It was some hours after the last of the energetic nutrient-destroying displays that something unusual happened. Lehesu felt a tight, powerful beam of communications energy coming from the blockaded nebula entrance. While he knew the language, he didn't know the culture; the gulf between planet-bound species and free-fall dwellers was so enormous that *any* understanding was a gigantic tribute to the oswaft's intellectual capabilities. Whatever they were saying out there, it was frantic, and not at all friendly.

It happened again! Judging from the manner in which this second burst was all bunched up into the higher frequencies, something was headed away from the fleet and toward the ThonBoka, fast. Lehesu maneuvered that way, both by straightforward distance-covering flight to keep an "eye" on the incoming signals, and by nonlinear distance-avoiding hops. Whatever was coming, it ought to have *some* kind of reception committee.

Suddenly an impossibly solid bar of unbearably bright light lashed out, connecting the two points in space with each other. There was a brilliant flash, a scattering of reflections, then nothingness. A sparkling hint of metallic debris and smoke lingered at the very edge of Lehesu's sensory capabilities. The galactic drift carried traces of scorched titanium and plastic into the ThonBoka.

A long, quiet moment followed. Then, without warning, something materialized not far from Lehesu, out of the wherever-it-is that starships go when they're traveling faster than the speed of light.

It was an absurdly shaped object, like something resembling a coral-encrusted horseshoe magnet a tenth the oswaft's size and possessing none of his fluid grace. The thing was tumbling slowly, end over end, while enormous volumes of dense white smoke billowed from its blast-blackened rear surface.

Naturally, Lehesu recognized her at once.

"Lando! Vuffi Raa! Can you hear me in there? Are you all right?"

The vacuum-breather swam closer, carefully avoiding the foul-smelling effluents issuing from the curved rear edge of the freighter. Nothing indicated that life had ever inhabited the strangely shaped craft. The glow-spots he now knew to be windows lay dark and foreboding along her surfaces as she continued to somersault gently before the space-going sentient, the random motion itself a grim presentiment that nothing rational lived at the controls.

"Vuffi Raa! Lando! Speak to me!" the oswaft beamed on every frequency he knew. "This is Lehesu!"

Nothing replied.

Much more figuratively than literally, Lehesu cast a backward glance at the Centrality fleet besieging his home. He didn't know how he could accomplish it, but he swore, in that moment of grief, a terrible revenge against those who were responsible for the tragedy. To gain and lose new friends, good friends—in some respects the only friends he'd ever had—in what seemed to the extremely long-lived creature like the mere space of minutes...It was almost more than a being could bear.

Thrashing frantically back and forth, he peered into the vessel's darkened ports, learning nothing. Gently, he nudged the spaceship, unintentionally adding an additional vector to her tumbling motion.

"Lando! Vuffi Raa! Are you in there?"

He thought a moment, then, despite everything he had struggled to understand about his new companions, added: "*Falcon*, my little friend, *please* talk to me! This is Lehesu the oswaft! Are Vuffi Raa and Lando still alive?"

EIGHT

THE REFITTED CRUISER *WENNIS* WAS A TROWEL-SHAPED
wedge of metal bristling with instrument and weapons
implacements arranged to overlap yet not interfere with
one another's fields of effectiveness. At an unusual—
and unusually heavily shielded—point on her after surface, between the great blinding arrays of drive tubes
and deflectors, was a small chamber with windowless
walls two meters thick. It could be entered only by a
small auxiliary craft, available to the vessel's master alone,
and then only when he had ordered the drives temporarily
shut down. To navigate the small craft while the cruiser's
massive engines were in operation would be instanta-
neous suicide.

Two hundred centimeters is a great deal of wall, especially when it is composed of the latest, state-of-the-
art battlewagon armor. Yet the armoring of the special
chamber was not intended to protect its contents from
the ravening drive radiations of the *Wennis*. It was to
protect the *Wennis* from what lay in the chamber. Even
so, it was a futile effort, intended more to comfort the
one entity who knew what the arrangement was all about,
to provide some sense, however illusory, of security.

Inside the chamber, Rokur Gepta stood before a chest-high metal pylon capped with a transparent bubble the size of a man's head. Gepta knew the chamber and controls by memory. No light burned within it. He ran a gray-gloved hand along the surface of the pylon, watching with unseeing eyes as his fingers pressed inset keys. Inside the bubble, he had begun to create an infinitessimal speck of the most dangerous single substance the universe had ever known. A sickly green light began to seep from the bubble, filling the darkened chamber with malignant luminosity.

The trouble with a man like Klyn Shanga, the sorcerer thought, wasn't that he was not afraid to die. It had taken Gepta an unprecedentedly long while to figure that out, so tortuous and alien was the line of reasoning involved. Rokur knew many individuals who were not fearful of death, in fact they seemed to welcome the idea, embrace the opportunity. They were eager to die, for their beliefs, for the Centrality or the numerous causes that opposed it, even for Gepta himself. Such men were easy to control and extremely useful. Down deep somewhere they hated and feared life and were anxious to be relieved of the burden of living in a manner that would not disturb their other, contradictory beliefs.

It was clear Klyn Shanga enjoyed being alive, which was what made things confusing. Rokur Gepta was not used to being confused, and it infuriated him. How was it that someone who loved life could be unafraid to die? The first conclusion the sorcerer had reached—not much help in understanding the perverse phenomenon, but of high pragmatic significance—was that the original Centrality expedition to Renatasia hadn't done a thorough enough job. They had done only two-thirds of it, and it badly wanted finishing.

Gepta promised himself to assign that matter the highest of priorities once the current operation was over and he could think about other things. If Shanga was representative of Renatasia's people, that system could turn out to be a much greater danger to his plans—and to the Centrality—than even the essentially harmless vacuum-breathers of the ThonBoka.

He gazed into the ghastly glow before him, savoring its destructive potential. One cubic millimeter of the substance, established in a self-sustaining manner, would leap from point to point on a planet's surface, eradicating anything that lived, devouring any organic substrate on which future life depended. It was the ultimate disinfectant, the ultimate sterilizer. There was something wonderfully clean and neat about this substance and the very concept of it.

It cleared up confusion. *Life* was confusion, and intelligent life the most contradictory and confusing of all, realized Gepta. Klyn Shanga wanted to live, yet was unafraid to die. Such a man could not be controlled, and, when he had something that the sorcerer wanted, he became...*impossible!* It had not been two hours since he interviewed the man, shortly after the *Wennis* met his ragtag squadron in deep space. The craft of Shanga's squadron were not interstellar vessels, and they were to have waited for Gepta at the edge of his home system. But so eager had they been for the ThonBoka (or desirous of leaving Tund) that they had departed early, confident the cruiser would overtake them before they ran into trouble.

"*It was insubordination!*" the livid Gepta hissed, looking down at Admiral Shanga. Their confrontation was not being held on the bridge because of the possibility that things would be said that would harm discipline.

Shanga threw his head back and laughed. "I am not your *subordinate*, magician, nor is the least senior of my men. We felt like going and we went. Here we are, closer to the ThonBoka than we would have been, the better rested for having done something constructive to get ourselves there. Is it this that you find objectionable?"

Beneath the bridge of the *Wennis* lay the captain's battle quarters, which, like his command chair, had also been preempted by the sorcerer. A duplicate of the command chair was placed in the center of the room before a large viewscreen, which presently showed the depths of interstellar space, as translated by the ship's computers from the hyperdrive hash of what was really to be seen. The light was gray and even, matching the sorcerer's clothing and, somehow, his voice.

"You are a military man, Admiral, I oughtn't to need to explain these matters to you, of all people."

The military man grinned and shook his head. "I *was* a military man. Now I am a mercenary in my own employ, fighting, because it suits me to do so, for the honor of a civilization that no longer exists. I recognize no authority and I desire no authority. My men follow me because it suits them."

He grew tired of standing. The discussion was altogether too much like being called to the school supervisor's office, and it rankled. Shanga looked around, discovered a lounger beside the door to the corridor, tossed his helmet onto another chair, and reclined, stretching his customarily ship-cramped legs and relaxing.

Shanga groped around inside his spacesuit until he found tobacco in a shirt pocket. He withdrew the cigar, put it in his mouth, and lit it with a hundredth-power discharge of his blaster. Gepta's guards hadn't taken his weapon this time. He hadn't let them. Three of them had broken arms and a fourth, who'd gone on insisting, was dead. That was the real reason for the conference.

"Let's put our card-chips in the table-field, Gepta," Shanga said through a cloud of blue smoke. "You're up to something—the way you've redecorated this cruiser is evidence enough of that—and it amounts to more than simple revenge against one lousy gambler. And you need us. I've got twenty-three flyers in a battered assortment of fighters gathered from the scrap heaps of a dozen cultures, and yet any one of them is a match for any three of yours."

The sorcerer gripped the arms of his chair, convulsively fending off the impulse to have the man disintegrated where he sat. There was too much light in the room for his comfort, and increasingly too much smoke. Yet he had always prided himself on an ability, a willingness, to withstand temporary deprivation and discomfort for the sake of future gains. "Oh, and how is it that you reach this conclusion?" he asked evenly. After all, the crew of the *Wennis* was the best the Centrality had to offer.

Shanga blinked, considering his words. "It's how you throw away good people. Your whole culture places no value on the individual. Funny, because that's all there is: no 'group,' no 'navy,' no 'empire,' only individuals, who do all the thinking, all the work, that gets done. Waste that, and it'll come back to haunt you, Gepta. People aren't plug-in modules you can use up. That's why my guys are a match for any five Centrals. They know they're irreplaceable, and...Look: you've got a drive tech who's pretty good, but doesn't have the right family or connections, or espouses the wrong beliefs. Disregard his unique competence, pack him off to the life-orchards or the spice mines, and all that leaves you are the socially acceptable incompetents. Starts to show, after a while; the machinery grinds down."

A tiny portion of the gray-robed sorcerer that was

neither illusion nor altogether human shuddered. And controlled himself. Klyn Shanga's time would come later. In the meantime, in order to prevent morale-destroying rumors from spreading through the crew, he would order that "complications" set in among the lesser casualties of Shanga's intransigence. They'd be given space burial with full honors; he needed to shut down the ship's drives briefly, anyway.

"We shall agree," he said to the fighter pilot with forced amiability, "to disagree; it is not necessary that we hold the same philosophy in order to cooperate."

"No," Shanga nodded, "it isn't. What's important is that I have my squadron, you have this ship and passage through the Centrality fleet. Together, we both know Calrissian, have confronted him in the past. He'll become your prisoner—or worse. We'll have Vuffi Raa, the Butcher of Renatasia, to haul back in force shackles for public trial and execution!"

Knowing full well that a very different fate awaited the squadron commander—one not dissimilar to that which he planned for the gambler—Gepta nevertheless replied, "Yes, of course. Then you will be free to rebuild your civilization." A hint of cordiality very nearly made it into his tone.

"Rebuild Renatasia? There's nothing left *to* rebuild! We've become the stinking suburbs of your Centrality! Everything we have, everything we do is a pale, threadbare, plastic imitation of whatever was in fashion ten years ago in the capital! All we have left to aspire to is . . . *justice!*"

Inwardly, Gepta chuckled. How right the admiral was; how much more right he would be. The sorcerer watched Shanga for a moment, sitting in his presence without permission, *smoking*, and enjoyed the unintended irony. Then he pressed a button on one arm of his throne.

"You know Vuffi Raa, Admiral Shanga, and we both have reason to know Lando Calrissian." The name stuck unpleasantly in Gepta's throat; the two words were not the terms on which he was used to thinking of the man, but Shanga would not appreciate or understand the sorcerer's private system of references. "Now let us hear from one who claims to know something about what else awaits us in the ThonBoka, shall we?"

The squadron leader shrugged, looking suddenly old and tired. He needed to get back to his men. He needed—

A door slid aside, and a tall, gangly human being entered, a man with bushy white hair and a permanently sour expression pulled down over his long undertaker's features.

"Fleet Admiral Klyn Shanga of Renatasia," the sorcerer intoned formally, "Please meet the *Ottdefa* Osuno Whett, Associate Professor of Comparative Sapient Studies at the Centrality—"

"College boys, now!" the fighter pilot snorted, his energy renewed by contempt. "What's he got to contribute to this palaver, anyway?"

"Rather a good deal, my dear—Admiral, was it?" There was a note of polite disbelief in the man's voice as he examined Shanga's clothing, found a place to seat himself, looking first to Gepta for approval, and sat. "I am the galaxy's foremost expert—by virtue of the fact that I am the only expert, heh, heh—on the oswaft, the intelligent space-evolved life of the ThonBoka."

"Some expert! According to our friend the magician, here, nobody knew about those creepy-crawlies until a few months ago, nobody. How much could you have learned in—"

Whett looked a bit disturbed, as if Shanga's disrespect for Gepta, or at least its punishment, might be contagious. "Sir, I am an anthropologist, the very same who unrav-

♦ 76 ♦

eled the impenetrable mysteries of the Sharu of Rafa. I have lived among and studied the asteroid miners of the Oseon, I—"

"The way I heard it, Mister Associate Professor, the Sharu sort of unraveled themselves!" He blew a puff of smoke from his relit cigar and laughed, particularly to see that mention of the Sharu made even Rokur Gepta appear momentarily uncomfortable. Now *there* was a race of sorcerers!

"My title, *Admiral*, is *Ottdefa*, an honor conferred by my home system, and I would thank you to—"

"Forget it, friend, I got carried away." Shanga looked back to Gepta. He was one of the few men in the known galaxy who could look directly into the sorcerer's face without wincing. "Okay, I'll bite: what's this all about?"

Without a word, Gepta nodded at the *Ottdefa*, who began again.

"The oswaft are a most unusual people. I began observing them with an electronic telescope, at the behest of Lord Gepta, until it became apparent that they were aware of the instrument's emanations. Then, in a specially fitted meteoroid, I traversed much of their region, making observations with less intrusive devices. They evolved in space, out of the clutter of organic molecules to be found there, and reached the pinnacle of intelligence, protected by the nebula that all but encloses them, and unaware that anyone else existed.

"They have a natural ability to enter hyperspace and travel through it. They communicate by modulating radio-frequency waves with their brains. Theirs is a complex, highly sophisticated language, and it is just about all the culture they possess. They have no need of clothing or shelter, and what little food they require drifts past them on a sort of breeze. Hence, they make few artifacts, most of them sculptures or bodily decorations."

Shanga shook his head. "I don't get it. It's stupid enough that the navy is bothering with them. From everything you say, they're no threat to anybody; they don't want anything anybody has. But what's the point of *our* boning up on—"

"Because, my dear Shanga," the sorcerer hissed, "they are allies to our enemies! We shall either win them over and force them to betray Calrissian, or they, too, shall be destroyed!"

Now, in his special secret chamber aft of the *Wennis'* drives, Rokur Gepta contemplated the temporary contents of a force-bubble stronger than the full battle-shielding of the cruiser. Perched upon its pylon, it contained a secret an entire race, the Sorcerers of Tund, had died to protect.

At greater strength now, its ghostly flicker filled the room with evil dancing shadows, all of them Gepta's. He felt at peace. It was the only light he really liked. It reminded him of home. The home he had remodeled with its assistance.

Inside the bubble tiny forms seethed and sizzled at the border of visibility, like dust motes in a sunbeam. They were densest at the bottom of the bubble, yet many thousands more sparkled in the space above the bottom. They were lively, active, *hungry*.

Gepta chuckled to himself. In a manner of thinking, they, too, were his pets. He had harnessed the most dangerous forces in the universe and kept them there in a cage. He made and unmade them at his pleasure. And he had work for them to do. Again. There was enough . . . substance . . . there to eliminate the life in an entire globular cluster.

The ThonBoka, all its inhabitants, Lando Calrissian, Vuffi Raa, Klyn Shanga—yes, and perhaps this arm of the Centrality navy, which was, after all, another obstacle to his desire for power—all of them would feel the agony of first contact with this, the most unusual of all his pets.

And then they would feel nothing.

He shut off the switches. Where there had been activity before within the bubble, all movement stopped. The green glow died abruptly. The motes stopped dancing. It was drawing near the time that Gepta had arranged to have the drives shut down again, so that he could steer his small auxiliary through the zone of murderous radiation, back to the main hull of the *Wennis*.

The force-bubble grew smaller until it, too, disappeared, leaving the smooth, mirror-surface top of the pylon, a simple pedestal of polished metal. Gepta smiled to himself, pocketed the one small object he had removed from the pedestal as the force-field deactivated, and began cycling the airlock.

How beautiful to contemplate an entire galaxy of worlds glowing sweetly thus, to imagine the whole universe clean and sterile, linear and predictable.

The One said to the Other, "I observe that you have brought the Rest."

They were arrayed before him, rank on rank, less for the sake of discipline (a concept utterly alien to those beings) or even orderliness, than for the simple reason that all of them wanted to see and hear what was going to happen next. Uncountable numbers of them bristled with unfamiliar tenseness. They were not altogether certain it was an improvement over their normal state.

"Yes," confirmed the Other, like his companion, like all his companions, glittering in the cold diamond starlight, "and I believe that they wish for you to address them now, explain—"

"But they know as well as you or I," the One protested,

rude interruptions and strained emotions coming now with greater frequency, even at so vast a remove from their grand experiment. "They're all perfectly familiar with—"

"Yes," his friend said, but gently, "and yet they wish it as a kind of ceremony, marking the passage of one epoch and the initiation of another, unknown, somehow frightening one. I wish it, too, if you do not mind greatly."

The One hesitated, even though he had already assented within himself. After all, if those he cared for felt the need . . . and perhaps it would help calm him, as well. What sort of result would issue when this project was mature, however, worried him. Already circumstances were nearly unbearable.

"My friends, as we all know, some while ago, a rather long time, even for we who are perhaps the most longevous race in the galaxy, at my suggestion we caused a being to come into existence among us who was, well, somewhat different, imbuing him certain minor physical advantages, and a burning desire to know about the universe."

There was a murmuring of remembrance, a stir of suppressed excitement. Change was coming hard and fast to the One, the Other, and the Rest.

"This being was peaceful, unaggressive even by our standards, for we had shaped him in this wise for several reasons that made sense to us and still do. Nonetheless, he has become embroiled in one violent incident after another, brutal, sanguine clashes with primitive cultures. Lives have been lost.

"Yet he has learned much, and the time has arrived for us to learn it from him."

The rumbling of comment from the Rest grew louder. The One gave them time to contemplate, then said at last, "We go now to gather him in. We do not even know whether he will be happy to see us, to learn that his searches, at least for the time being, are over with. Let us greet him in dignity and love, understand the trials he has been through, and treasure what he has to give us, for it is rich.

"And it will change everything."

NINE

TUMBLING PONDEROUSLY BOW OVER STERN, AND WITH the slightest of rolls to starboard, the *Millennium Falcon* slowed microscopically, her attitude burners sputtering at irregular intervals in the eternal darkness. Her roll corrected, her pitch losing its momentum, she stablized and came to a full stop. There was a fitful, uncertain fluttering of red at her ports, scattered here and there around her battered hull, then the strong, clear crimson of emergency lighting.

From small jets at the rear, streams of milky liquid struck her after hull plates, boiling off noiselessly in thick, gaseous clouds that mingled with the trailing smoke. A still-molten stub of structural metal projecting to the precise edge of her shield radius cooled and dimmed. The smoke ceased pouring; the interior lights and running markers came on full.

From a pressure valve in the circular hatch atop the *Falcon*'s hull, a mast extruded, silvery, slender, obviously being paid out by hand in jerky increments. It stopped with a springy quiver when two meters of it were visible. Lehesu, floating nearby, heard a familiar voice:

"Hello there, old flatfish! Lost the main antenna in

all the excitement back there! That is you, isn't it, Lehesu? Glad to be here. If Vuffi Raa had hesitated by a picosecond, you'd be talking to our radioactive ghosts!"

From a rather different culture—one, for example, whose conception of death did not encompass fancies of an ectoplasmic afterlife—Lehesu failed to comprehend at least two-thirds of the greeting. Nevertheless, he understood that his friends had safely arrived in the ThonBoka, and was overjoyed.

"Landocaptainmaster!" the vacuum-breather exclaimed, unconsciously addressing the human occupant of the starship as an oswaft Elder, "Yes, it is I!" He swam closer to the spacecraft until he could peer into its control room through the canopy. Inside sat Lando Calrissian, con man and sometime gambler (or gambler and sometime con man), and his mechanical would-be servant, Vuffi Raa. Full-time robot.

The two were still busily turning knobs and pushing buttons, attempting to restore the *Millennium Falcon* to some semblance of operational normality. The captain's seat harness lay unfastened, floating in the temporarily gravity-free air about his acceleration couch. So it had been he, most probably, who had erected the antenna, aft and upstairs. The young oswaft was pleased to have deduced the data, insignificant as they might be. It meant he was beginning to have a feel for what had been a totally alien environment and civilization.

"Greetings and salutations, friend Lehesu," the droid echoed. *"Not one of my better entrances, I'm afraid. And we both apologize for the delay in reaching you."* He looked to Lando, who was nodding, although whether in assent to the apology or as a comment on the robot's flying skills was moot. *"We were within hailing distance,"* Vuffi Raa continued, *"of the Starcave, several*

days ago, but it was necessary to work our way through the blockading fleet by means of deception."

There was the slightest hint of distaste in the robot's voice, Lando thought. It annoyed him; deception was supposed to be one of his major stocks-in-trade, and Vuffi Raa understood that as well as anyone. Besides, how else were they supposed to have gotten through the fleet? He lit a cigar and gazed out through the wedge-sectioned port at the oswaft floating gently ahead of the motionless *Falcon*. Centrality blockade or not, it was good to be out of circulation, beyond the reach of what passed for civilization—and of hired assassins—however temporarily. Knowing the navy, he had a pessimistic notion just how safe they were within the nebula and for how long. But he had a plan for that, too, and encouraged by his relatively easy victory over the fleet thus far, he intended to relax.

"*I do not understand*," Lehesu protested in response to something Vuffi Raa had said when Lando wasn't listening. "*I believed that I had seen you and the* Falcon *utterly destroyed. Of course, at the time, I didn't know it was you, but . . .*"

Satisfaction suffused the droid's tone, "It was my master's idea, really. During the time I described to you, while he was spying upon the enemy under the guise of selling things and gambling, I fitted out a cylinder of powdered metallic shavings mixed with various volatiles, and attached it to the stern of the *Falcon*. This we left unshielded, so that the cruiser's rays, upon striking it, would convey the illusion that . . ."

I wonder what we would have done if they'd simply used a tractor beam, Lando mused. He'd counted on the guns' being manned by trigger-happy jerks, and, as usual, he'd been right. For a while he watched Lehesu, not really paying attention as that being and the little droid communicated. They seemed to get along automatically, he thought, had little trouble achieving understanding. Idly, he wondered why. For all the goodwill in the galaxy, he had to struggle to identify with a creature who had never known a planet's surface, for whom empty space was a comfortable home, who could shift light-years at a time within it, somehow avoiding the necessity for those careful computations the gambler had learned so painfully as an inexperienced captain.

Against the charcoal backdrop of the nebula, a handful of stars twinkled merrily through the transparent innards of the space being. Lando laughed, dismissing every doubt and trouble he was feeling with a shake of his head, took another drag on his cigar through a wide grin, then rose from his seat.

"Pardon me, old gumball machine, if you can, but I'm going aft to change into my bathing togs. Care to join me?" Without waiting for a reply, he stubbed out the cigar and pulled himself between the jumpseats toward the rear of the cockpit.

The robot stirred from his conversation with the oswaft. "If I interpret you correctly, Master, I think I should like that very much." His five chromium-plated tentacles glittered over the control panels. "I shall inform our friend, and place the ship on automatic."

"Swell. Don't call me master."

Ducking through the doorway, Lando floated along the corridor until he reached a locker where he changed from the well-worn shipclothes he'd been wearing for the navy's benefit, into a spacesuit. By the time he'd sealed all the fittings and run through the checklist programmed into it, Vuffi Raa, who hadn't needed to change, caught up with him. Together they made their way to the airlock and cycled out through it into the void.

Lehesu was there to meet them.

It was the gambler's first good look at the ThonBoka from the inside, and the sight was eerie. Behind him, the nearly circular mouth of the nebula displayed the sky as he was accustomed to seeing it, a dense scattering of stars—with the occasional intrusion of an eruption of destructive energies from the fleet.

Everywhere else, the gas and dust shut out the rest of the universe with a solid wall of deep gray that appeared slightly phosphorescent, and through which gigantic bolts of lightning played intermittent natural counterpoint to the unnatural discharges from the navy. The eye, perhaps the mind itself, violently rejected proper proportions in that place. Lando knew that he was gazing across a dozen light-years, something like ten trillion kilometers, to the opposite wall, in reality a finite region of diffuse particles that would be scarcely noticeable to those aboard a ship traveling through it. His eyes told him he was near the entrance to an enormous but comprehensibly sized cavern, one that might require several days to traverse on foot, but a cavern nevertheless.

Billows and folds in the nebula resembled geologic flows, sheets of lime-stone deposition. All that was missing were stalagmites and stalactites. Illumination was provided by three small planetless blue-white stars that shone in the center of the Starcave, their photon pressure probably accounting for its hollow form, but not for their own presence. One star might have been sensible. Three, spaced a light-year or two apart, would have physicists making excuses to one another well into the next century. Lando was happy to be a gambler, a profession where alibis don't count. Biologists would be unhappy, too— or ecstatic—at the strange life that had evolved in the sheltered space.

Fingering colored plastic control buttons set into a small panel on the arm of his spacesuit, Lando jetted away from the upper hull and retroed to a floating halt a daring few meters away from the impressive young oswaft. It was something like greeting an ocean liner politely. He circumnavigated the five-hundred-meter creature in a smooth arc, tucked himself into a roll, straightened, and sprang away with arms extended wide, legs spread, and an expression of sudden joy on his face.

"*Yaaahooo!*" he whooped uncharacteristically, rejoicing in the sensation of free movement, open space. He realized he'd been cooped up aboard ship far too long. It felt like his entire life. Or perhaps evolving on a planet, squeezed between the ground and low-hanging sky, made one feel permanently claustrophobic.

Vuffi Raa, propelled by the Core alone knew what, spun like a bright metallic snowflake beside him as Lehesu rotated majestically, then veered off in a huge graceful curve the two smaller beings attempted to emulate. One of them succeeded.

"*Hey, you guys, wait for me!*" Lando shouted unnecessarily; his suit radio carried perfectly well over the kilometer or two he'd missed intercepting them by. Correcting, he tumbled slightly—the free-fall equivalent of tripping over his own feet—stabilized, and swooped to join his friends. By which time, of course, they were somewhere else.

Lando didn't care. On his own, he began essaying ancient patterns, maneuvers that, elsewhere and elsewhen, would be called Luftberry circles, Immelmann turns, imitating the inspired antics of fighting aerocraft of the prespace eras of every culture momentarily infatuated with free flight and glorious death. He dived on Lehesu, showering the vacuum-breather with imaginary reciprocating gun bullets, then pulled up at the last instant as the startled being instinctively rolled to peel the attacking foe off his back.

That didn't save Vuffi Raa. The unfortunate droid was sitting squarely in the bull's-eye etching of Lando's helmet—ordinarily used for the more mundane purpose of orienting oneself before setting off one's suit propellants—when Lando's deadly pointed fingers filled him full of hot-jacketed lead. Caught up in the spirit of the thing, the robot spun out and downward, wishing he could trail smoke for his master's amusement. There were limits, however, even to Vuffi Raa's remarkable capabilities.

Three small blue-white suns glowed against a somber dark-gray backdrop. Lightning licked the folds and billows of the cavern walls.

Three odd beings, oswaft, droid, and, oddest of all, human, passed an endless hour or so, playing at combat like the young of all intelligent life everywhere. It was both a release and a return at the same time, marred only by the momentarily suppressed dread of what lay outside the Starcave—and the sudden flare of baleful energy as the Centrality fleet, on its clockwork schedule of mass murder, sprayed poison and lethal power into the space around the ThonBoka mouth.

Lando cut his spin—that time, *he* had been the victim of Vuffi Raa's machine guns—and halted, hanging in space, resenting being catapulted back into adulthood, watching the stupidily unnecessary fleet operations with an angry grimace clearly visible through his transparent bubble helmet. Life was so simple, he thought bitterly, so thoroughly enjoyable. Why were there always people whose chosen profession was to louse it up for everybody else?

Vuffi Raa swam up beside the gambler, not needing to be telepathic to read his master's thoughts. They were joined by Lehesu. All three stared out through the mouth of the nebula, watching the evil net of beams that did its work of making life impossible for the oswaft. All knew of the enzymes drifting into the ThonBoka, as well.

"The nutrient current grows impoverished, my friends," Lehesu observed sadly. He was not actually breathing heavily from the hour's exercise, but the effect was much the same. Lando and Vuffi Raa didn't know his kind quite well enough to understand it was a bad sign.

"Core forgive me!" Lando exclaimed, "I'd almost forgotten why we came here in the first place!" He turned toward the *Millennium Falcon*, applied thrust to his suit. "We'll get you a little snack, old skate, then you can show us where best to place the rest of our cargo."

The robot and the man scooted underneath the starship, began manipulating the locks on a small cargo hatch. In a moment, clinging to the hull, they had it open and delivered of a small canister that Vuffi Raa held out.

"Here you are," Lando heard through his helmet phones. *"Shall I just spray it around, or would you prefer—"*

"That will be quite suitable, my friend, and many thanks." Lehesu tried hard to keep hunger out of his voice. He hadn't noticed until now how famished he'd become. As the specially selected amino acids and other compounds began drifting around the ship, he moved slowly and with dignity, scooping them up and ingesting them. He could feel them sing through his body and knew a joy akin to that which Lando felt at the prospect of freedom.

"Well, I certainly trust you're enjoying yourself in your selfish gluttony!"

It was a strange new voice over the ether, one incomprehensible to Lando, but Vuffi Raa understood it—and correctly interpreted its hostile tone. Both of them jetted quickly out from under the hull of the *Falcon*, which was blocking their view, as a pair of titanic monsters slid casually alongside, making even Lehesu appear small and meek.

He may not have had the robot's talent for languages, but the air of sarcastic disapproval hadn't been missed by the gambler, either. Reflexively, he patted the spacesuit pocket where he kept his stingbeam—then laughed inwardly at himself as he thought of pitting its miniscule power against these . . . these . . .

"These are the Elders you told us about, Lehesu?" he asked finally. "Tell them we're here to help them, and that, at the very least, we mean them absolutely no harm." He removed his hand from the pocket and tried to sound sincere.

And almost succeeded.

Easily seven hundred meters from wingtip to wingtip, the pair of oswaft dwarfed the *Falcon*, and everything else in view. They positioned themselves on either side of Lando's younger vacuum-breathing friend, as if that worthy were being arrested. Or sent to bed without his dinner.

"No," Lehesu replied in words the gambler could understand, *"these are most assuredly not the Elders, and they have no right or authority to interfere with us. Elders are much larger."*

He'd directed the final comment to the two interlopers. Apparently it was some kind of insult, although it was probably lost on the pair, spoken as it had been in human language, Lando thought. If Elders were even larger than these creatures, the gambler reflected, he certainly didn't want to mess with them.

Vuffi Raa put on a burst of speed, whipped around as if to block the progress of the three giant beings—as if a microbe could block the progress of a Bantha. *"I suggest,"* the droid radiated in a businesslike tone, *"that you be civil to our friend Lehesu, for he has performed a great service for you and the rest of your—"*

"Silence, insignificant one!" one of the creatures replied. *"You know not of what you speak. We are here at the explicit request of the Elders themselves. The three of you are to come to them at once, in order to explain your impertinence and face their mighty judgment!"*

TEN

"*S*ABACC!" CRIED LANDO CALRISSIAN, GAMBLER, CON *artiste*, and interstellar diplomat. He sat back on sheer nothingness with a satisfied look on his face and let the *Millennium Falcon* gather in his winnings, shuffle the "deck," and deal out the "card-chips" once again. It was the weirdest and most profitable game he'd ever played.

Senwannus'gourkahipaff, senior Elder of the oswaft, let a little ticklish signal be broadcast, indicating amusement and pleasure. *"Truly it is amazing, Captainmasterlandocalrissian."* Lando gave a mental shrug: if the head vacuum-breather wished to address him with a title longer than his own, indicating deep respect and a relaxed sort of submission, the gambler wasn't going to correct him. There was far too much at stake, and it had very little to do with the game of *sabacc*. *"Amazing,"* the thousand-meter being continued, *"you cannot even see the cards, yet you have won hand after hand under fair and impartial conditions. I abase myself to your skill and intellect."*

Lando congratulated himself a little, too, principally on his luck. They were playing in the center of the Cave of the Elders, the only architectural structure, as far as he knew, within the ThonBoka, very probably the only such the oswaft had ever constructed. Or thought to construct.

Located in the middle of the triangular plane formed by the three blue-white stars in the center of the nebula, the Cave of the Elders was a meticulous replica of the Starcave itself. From where he sat—hung might be a better word, as they were relaxing in free-fall—he could make out the folds and tucks he'd seen outside, duplicated in exact detail a mere ten kilometers away. A circular doorway repeated the pattern of the mouth of the ThonBoka (*sans*, he was happy for small favors, the Centrality fleet), and what he'd seen of the detail outside spoke exceptionally well for the inferential powers of the oswaft. With the exception of the adventurous Lehesu, they had never actually seen the outside of their nebula, yet they knew just what it had to look like.

The only flaw observable in the titanic modeling effort, and what made the Cave of the Elders *really* interesting, was that it was constructed entirely, all twenty klicks of its diameter, of precious gems.

From outside the entrance of the Cave, the *Falcon*'s computers pinged in his helmet phones, indicating two cards each had been dealt to Sen (Lando irreverantly abbreviated the being's name for the sake of his overworked tongue muscles), to Feytihennasraof, the second Elder, on the senior's left, and to Lehesu, who was also sitting in.

"You have a Three of Staves and a Commander of Sabres, Master," Vuffi Raa informed him from the ship, *"total value, fifteen."* The others would be "seeing" their cards by means of television signals produced by the computer. He wished the robot would let him count his own cards, almost as much as he wished the robot would stop calling him master, but there didn't seem to be much he

could do about it. To protect the privacy of Lando's hand, they spoke in Old High Trammic, the ancient language of the Toka/Sharu of the Rafa System.

The oswaft were too polite to mention that they'd "decoded" the language within five minutes of the game's beginning. They'd play fair in any case, ignoring the robot's signals. Both the translation and the refusal to take advantage were reflexive with the creatures; none of them had thought about the matter consciously. Honor and solving puzzles were instinctive with them.

"*I'll take one card,*" Sen intoned, indicating thanks once the *Falcon* had electronically dealt it. Fey, too, required a card, while the precocious Lehesu stood pat. Lando asked for a card, receiving Moderation, a minus fourteen, which made his hand worth one point.

"*Master, the computer has randomly altered your last card to an Eight of Flasks! That means—*"

"*Sabacc!*" Lando said before the robot could finish. That made a hundred and eighty million credits the oswaft owed him, if he'd kept his accounts straight. If he ever got out of that mess, life was going to be very, very different.

"*This is a most diverting occupation,*" Fey said. "*Shall we have another hand, Captainmasterlandocalrissiansir?*"

Swell: he'd been promoted by a syllable. At that rate, it would take all day to say his name. Maybe he should contrive to lose a few hands. It wouldn't be easy, seeing that the computer was actually controlling the cards, but he'd think of something.

Just like he had when they'd been summoned to confront the Elders.

Authority comes in many packages, and the contents seem to vary just as much as the outer trappings. Centrality power was based on naked, lethal, brute force, pure and simple and no shilly-shallying. The position of decision-makers in the Oseon, to choose just one example, depended on wealth. In the Rafa System, some deference seemed to be paid to religious leadership, although in that system, things were so tied up in ancient science that what looked like high priests might actually be senior technicians.

The oswaft were a conservative people. They deferred to age and experience. Lando had tried to ascertain how old the oswaft got to be, but couldn't. Like many lower species, they kept on growing throughout their lives. Lehesu was a young adult, say the equivalent of late teens or early twenties. He was about five hundred meters across the wingtips, and growing.

The pair of yes-men who'd picked them up near the ThonBoka mouth were apparently of middle years (or centuries or millennia), seven or seven hundred fifty meters in diameter and set in their ways. They hadn't much liked calling on tiny strangers or having tiny strangers calling on them, and they'd liked it less that a youngster like Lehesu had gone and changed the nice, smooth, boring flow of life in the Starcave.

The three adventurers had pointed out that Lando and Vuffi Raa couldn't simply go swimming off to meet the Elders. Lehesu wasn't prepared to say what would happen if he attempted to transport them as he had his nutrient cylinder back in the foodless desert. Nor was Lando prepared to risk such a venture. With some haggling, the pair of outsiders was permitted to return to the *Falcon* where, with faster-than-light drives activated, they followed the oswaft down into the hollow center of the nebula.

Under the triple suns of the Starcave, the Cave of the Elders was an impressive sight, glittering and gleaming from billions of points as it rotated slowly. Vuffi Raa, using the ship's sensors, informed the gambler that there wasn't a valuable stone in the known galaxy that wasn't represented in huge quantities in the walls of the Cave. Moreover, the size of the gems would have sent a jeweler into a dead faint.

Senwannus'gourkahipaff and Feytihennasraof had awaited them within the Cave of the Elders. Lehesu, with his excellent grasp of Lando's language, had spelled the names for the gambler and the robot, explaining that the apostrophe in Sen's name represented another dozen or so minor syllables the Elder was too modest to insist upon, and that there was a third Elder around somewhere who was busy and would join them later.

"Our most cordial greetings, Captainmasterlando" had been Sen's first words in the new form of speech Lehesu had taught the Elder in a matter of seconds. *"I abjure you to forgive the somewhat overzealous invitation issued to you by our juniors."*

The senior Elder administered a mental nudge of admonishment to the pair—a maser bolt that would have holed the *Falcon*, deflectors and all.

"Think nothing of it, Senwannus'gourkahipaff, your Eldership; they're not the first underlings to get carried away with borrowed authority. What can we do for you?"

"We are," Fey replied, *"given to understand that you have brought nutrients to replace those being destroyed by others of your kind outside the Starcave. Is this correct?"*

Lando nodded, a gesture he wasn't sure the oswaft could see or understand. They'd left the *Falcon* parked outside—although now he wondered why he'd bothered as there was plenty of room for her in the Cave—and jetted in to meet the Elders. "That's right, sir. Not very much, but it's only a beginning. And besides, I think I've figured out a way to get the Centies off your back."

"*But why should you bother yourself?*" Fey asked. "*And why should you oppose the actions and interests of your own kind in this matter? I'm afraid we do not understand you, Captainmaster, and until we do, we cannot accept this gift you offer.*"

The Elders were at least a kilometer across, Fey being slightly smaller than Sen. Lando felt silly negotiating with them—it was rather like carrying on a conversation with a large apartment building. But from earlier conversations with Lehesu, he was prepared for their attitude and these very questions.

"Well, aside from the fact that Vuffi Raa and I have grown rather fond of young Lehesu, here, we consider it a sort of a game." Lando wished, as he hung in space beside the huge raylike creature, that there was some provision for smoking a cigar in a spacesuit. He felt better making business talk if he could smoke.

"*A game? Please explain what you mean.*"

"Sure, Sen. I understand that you folks like mental puzzles. Well, my folks do, too. Only we've found a way to make them more interesting and challenging: we turn them into *games*. That's where somebody else tries to solve the puzzle first or better, or opposes your solution of it while he tries to work out his own."

"*Fascinating,*" Sen mused, almost to himself. He turned to Fey. "*Have you ever conceived of such a thing?*"

No answer came from the Elder. To a being so ancient, a new concept came as something of a shock.

"Right," Lando said, jetting closer to the pair of aliens. "And just to make it more fascinating, we try to play for something a little better than the sheer joy of solving the puzzle."

"*Such as what?*" both Elders said at once.

"Well, permit me to demonstrate, friends. Now take the game of *sabacc* . . ."

"Am I missing something obvious here," Lando offered conversationally as he took another "card" and the others considered their hands, "or are you people completely resigned to dying?"

A pale pink tinge suffused through Lehesu at Lando's boldness toward the Elders, but he kept his peace, trusting the gambler. Sen and Fey both performed the equivalent of looking up from their cards. Lando's helmet indicators said he was being brushed lightly by twin radar beams.

He knew the beings were far from stupid. Their transparent bodies made it easier and more difficult at the same time to figure out their internal arrangements, but from what he'd seen, he guessed that about two-thirds of their mass was brain, and pretty astute brain at that.

"Ah yes," Sen answered finally, *"that was the reason you were demonstrating* sabacc *to us. I had become so fascinated with the game itself, I had quite forgotten that its purpose was explaining why you wished to help us. So, you play a great* sabacc *game with your own kind out there, and we are a part of it. No, my friend, we do not wish to die, but there seems little alternative. I'll take a card, Starshipmillenniumfalcon, if you please."*

The ship, apparently unimpressed that it had been granted status not only as a person but as an Elder among the oswaft, duly blipped out a signal representing one of the seventy-eight *sabacc* cards, and fell silent again.

"There are plenty of alternatives, friend, there always are. The first, of course, is that you can give up and die. I'm glad to hear you reject it. That's a beginning, anyway. *Sabacc!* That makes twenty-three million you owe me. Can we take a break? I have to visit certain facilities aboard my ship, and we can carry on this conversation from there."

He jetted across the Cave of the Elders, leaving the oswaft behind, climbed onto the hull of the *Falcon* and into the airlock hatch, where Vuffi Raa greeted him. "Patch the intercom into the ship-to-ship, will you? I need a cigar to think properly, and the powwow has reached a critical point."

"Yes, Master, I've been listening. What are we going to do with twenty-three million credits worth of precious stones? I don't believe we have room in the—"

"We'll figure that out when there's a point to it. Right now staying alive gets top priority." He'd unsealed his helmet and hung it on a rack, and, retaining the rest of his suit, climbed down into the lounge, where for once he left the gravity on, enjoying the feel of some weight under him.

"The second alternative," he continued, once contact was reestablished, "is to fight. You folks have some impressive talents; your size alone is pretty terrifying, at least for people of my size, but I think—"

"*Captainmasterlandocalrissian,*" interrupted Sen, "*we are not a fighting people, in fact the concept is nearly as new to us as that of gaming—and somewhat related, I would guess. In any event, there is a third way . . .*"

"And what would that be?" the gambler asked as he slowly and deliberately singed the business end of a cigar, keeping the flame well away from the tip.

"*Negotiation. You will recall mention of a third Elder, Bhoggihalysahonues? At this moment, she and a delegation of other oswaft have appeared at the mouth of the Starcave and are signaling for a peace-conference with your fleet. We wish to ask upon what terms—*"

"You bet your apostrophe I remember Boggy, and I can predict *exactly* what's going to happen, Sen. The navy wants you dead, old beanbag, and that's the only terms they're going to settle for. I've seen their work on other occasions, and you can believe me when I—"

"This is much what I had surmised," the second Elder said, *"and I opposed the attempt, yet we are an open and free people and would not prevent our third Elder from trying what she might. Yet you have mentioned other alternatives to dying, fighting, and negotiating."*

"There's running away."

"What, and leave the ThonBoka?" So much emotion loaded the response that Lando couldn't tell which oswaft it had come from. He poured himself a glass of fruit juice (spacesuits tend to dehydrate one a bit) and sat back down, puffing on his cigar. Vuffi Raa was forward, keeping his big red eye on the controls. It was difficult but important to remember that they were still in deep space. He could see how the oswaft thought of the place as a safe haven.

"I don't know," he said at last. "I gather from Lehesu's experiences that you folks aren't biologically tied to the place. It's an alternative to dying, isn't it?"

A long, long silence ensued while the massive brains outside processed his heresy. Finally: *"I am not sure, Lando, that it is a desirable alternative. We are the ThonBoka; the Thonboka is the oswaft. Would you willingly be driven out of your home, accept an eternity of wandering—"*

He laughed. "Sen, I accepted wandering as a way of life a long time ago. It beats the Core out of working for a living." The gambler mused. There were a lot of strange life-forms in the galaxy, ranging, in the matter of size alone, from these gigantic creatures, the largest he'd ever heard of, down to the tiny Crokes of . . . well, something-or-other. He couldn't remember the system. What made it interesting was that in his travels he'd observed that the biggest critters were almost invariably the most gentle and timid. Well, it made sense: if you were little, you had to learn to be tough. If you were big, it didn't matter. He guessed he'd always thought of himself as somewhere in the middle.

"Okay, yeah. Well, what if you appeared to do one or another of these things—sort of like the way I taught you to bluff in *sabacc*? Say you looked like you were going to destroy the fleet. Or, say you looked like you were all dead? I hate to bring up a touchy subject, but Lehesu tells me you folks sort of disintegrate when you die, drift away in a cloud of dust?"

Another long, uncomfortable silence. At long last, the daring Lehesu spoke for his Elders. *"That's correct, Lando, we return to our constituent molecules. Not the happiest of thoughts. Why, is it important?"*

Finishing his cigar, Lando stood, walked back to the ladder and up to the airlock, screwed on his helmet, and went outside. The Cave of the Elders floated beside the *Falcon* like a fantastic decorated egg, a million brilliant colors, a billion gleaming facets. He drifted toward the entrance and faced the three giant beings who waited for him there.

"Yes, it could be very important. It means you don't leave any remains behind that can be detected against the normal molecular background of space. It means they won't be looking for any stiffs."

"Stiffs?" the three said at once.

"Bodies, corpses, DOAs, meat, Qs—*corpora delicti*. Tell me, what are conditions like out by the wall of the Starcave?"

If oswaft had been capable of blinking at a rapid change of subject, Sen, at least, would have done so. *"Why, not terribly different from here. A bit colder, but not uncomfortably so."*

"Vuffi Raa," Lando said into the radio in his suit, "get me some scanning data on the nebula wall, will you? I've been working on an idea. Sen, Fey, Lehesu, can you people get *through* the wall at all?"

Lehesu replied, being the only one with any practical experience in the matter. "It is all but impenetrable. One cannot—what is your expression?—'starhop' because one cannot see where one is going. It is said that attempting it in any case will cause one to burst into flame and vanish."

Lando considered this. "Makes sense. No matter how diffuse the gas and dust is, translight speeds will create that kind of friction. How deep could you—what is your expression?—'swim' into the wall if you had to? Far enough so that sensors couldn't detect you?"

It was Lehesu's turn to think. While he was doing so, a sudden burst of radio transmissions entered the Cave of the Elders. It caused some stir. Lando couldn't understand what was being said, but no one interrupted the conversation for a translation, so the gambler put it out of his mind.

At long last: *"Yes, I believe such might be possible. If I follow your line of reasoning, you would have us conceal ourselves, we and all of the oswaft, within the folds and billows of the wall until the Centrality fleet, believing in their despicable villainy that we had starved to death, gave up and went away to impose misfortune upon someone else. But what would you have us do about the molecular residue that—"*

The gambler grinned. "I have that all figured out, my overlarge friend. It wouldn't take very much, would it? How about a little of my cargo, judiciously sprayed all over the place?"

"Lando! I believe the idea might work. Esteemed Elders, may I ask—"

"Silence, young one. Peace! We have something else to ponder at this moment, something very disturbing."

"What's happening, Sen, what's going on?"

The giant spoke: "*Bhoggihalysahonues*' attempts to negotiate an end to these insane hostilities have ended in disaster! She, and all of her party—a thousand of our people—were murdered with energy-weapons almost the moment they appeared at the mouth of the ThonBoka and greeted the nearest vessel."

"I'm sorry to hear it, Sen . . . but, well, it doesn't really change things very much, does it?"

"*I am afraid, Captainmasterlandocalrissiansir, that it does. You see, unfortunately, and in their consternation—the details aren't very clear—the negotiation party shouted at the . . . 'cruiser,' much as I did in an unthinking moment just now at the two oswaft who brought you here so ill-usedly.*"

"Yeah. *I* felt it, and it was a tight beam. The *Courteous*? What happened to her?" He had a bad feeling about this.

Sen gave the broadcast equivalent of a mournful sigh. "*She—your* Courteous *—was not well defended, as is your* Millennium Falcon, *by deflector-shields, for they thought our people harmless.*

"*Thus was the* Courteous *utterly destroyed.*"

"Swell," Lando said, more to himself than to the Elders. "Nothing like a premature war on our hands."

"*The rest of the fleet, with full shields up now, has entered the ThonBoka mouth to murder us all in retribution.*"

ELEVEN

Klyn Shanga grinned a humorless grin. "Well, Bern, you've really put your foot in it this time, old friend."

The wiry little man on the fold-down cot spread his skinny arms and shrugged, returning his commander's rueful smile. He wore a dark-green military shipsuit with a well-abraded band around the waist where he was used to carrying a gunbelt. Shanga's low-slung holster was likewise empty; no weapons were permitted in the cellblock of the *Wennis'* detention sector.

"You know what they say, Boss, sometimes you trick the sorcerer, sometimes the sorcerer tricks you." He pursed his lips, tongue protruding generously, and made a rude and juicy noise.

An alarmed look playing momentarily over his broad and deeply seamed features, Shanga glanced around reflexively for listening devices.

His smaller associate laughed. "What're they gonna do, throw me in the clink for insubordination? That'd be like jailing a murderer for littering." Harsh light from the naked overhead bulb reflected from the man's equally naked scalp. Where he did have hair, on the sides and back, it was clipped into a dirty gray stubble.

Shanga sat down on the cot beside his friend, extracted a pair of cigars from a pocket. There was a brief silence while they got them lit. "Well, I've got to admit, when you tried hijacking that auxiliary, you climbed pretty high on the wanted list. I wish to the Core you'd consulted me before you—"

"What, and have you wind up here, yourself? Boss, you *know* you'd have done the same thing I did. There are five pinnaces tucked away aboard this scow with the capability for faster-than-light travel, and our fighters can't hack it. If that blockade fleet moves in before we get to the nebula, we're gonna lose the Butcher!"

And our reason for living, Shanga thought, reading the same thoughts displayed on his friend's face. Bern Nuladeg was the only member of his squadron who went back with him to before his original retirement. They'd served their country together in a brief but bloody conflict with one of its neighbors, earning their wings, both of them becoming aces. When Shanga retired, Nuladeg had gone on to become a flight instructor, finally the commander of his nation-state's flight academy. The invasion from the stars had changed all of that.

Now they flew together in a squadron made up not only of their fellow countrymen but of personnel belonging to their former enemy, individuals from other nations, other planets in their system. They were all Renatasians, and they all wanted the same thing. Vengeance.

"I know, Bern, I know. That's why you did it on your own, didn't take any of the others along. You were going to steal that lighter yourself—then what?"

The small, bald-headed figure chuckled. "Hadn't gotten that far along in my plans. Days before we reach the ThonBoka at this speed, Klyn, *days*! What can Gepta be thinking of, permitting the invasion to begin before we get there? I heard the story—had the ring of truth to it—and acted. Guess I would have swung around and offered you fellows a ride, if I'd had the chance. I dunno. What're they gonna do to me, do you suppose?"

Shanga shook his head. "I have a meeting—an 'audience,' *he*'d like to style it—with our gray-robed cousin in an hour or so. We're going to talk about it then. I won't lie to you, it doesn't look good. You should see the way he treats his own people."

Nuladeg's laughter was practically a giggle now. "I know! That's what made swiping that machine so blasted easy: everybody was afraid to move for fear of getting terminally reprimanded! Whoever said dictatorship's efficient, Boss? It'd be funny if it weren't so downright stupid." He drew on his cigar, blew a smoke ring toward the bulb in the ceiling. Then his laughter died along with the smile creasing his face.

"Klyn, promise me one thing: don't worry about me enough to stop this mission. Whatever you do. I mean it. I can take whatever they dish out, but I can't stand the thought . . ."

Bern Nuladeg's entire family had been killed by Imperial troopers enjoying a few hours off-duty time. It had been a lark for them, and had only finished what they'd actually been guilty of. The field commander for the group had dismissed it as a prank—the same commander was found the next morning, in his own bed, with a Centrality-issue bayonet thrust through his lower jaw into his brain. No one had ever solved the mystery of how it had been done in a heavily guarded building on the grounds of the former flight academy, nor of who had done it or why.

"All right, old friend," Shanga sighed. He'd always thought that Nudaleg, who was the better pilot, experienced with command responsibility, ought to have been running the tattered squadron. The little man had refused even the number-two position, citing an impulsiveness that no one had truly believed in until now. "I'll see what I can do. You're right, I'm afraid. I was thinking about those pinnaces myself, when I heard about the moves against the Starcave. I'll see what I can do and be back with you as soon as possible."

He rapped loudly on the wall, pointedly ignoring the call button beside the force-fielded door. "Guards! Let me out of here! I have to see a toad about a man!"

A quarter of a galaxy away, the One, the Other, and the Rest raced to keep a rendezvous. They had come from even farther, and their speed was something no one in what Lando and his friends regarded as a civilization would have believed.

"We move so slowly!" the Other complained, plunging through hyperspace beside the One. "I fear we shall not get there on time!"

The One allowed himself to be distracted from his head-long course long enough to indicate a smile. "Impatience from you, after all this time, my friend? Truly, this is an era of changes. Never fear, we shall learn what we shall learn, regardless. I, too, would prefer that we—"

The Other interrupted. "Events move of their own accord! What shall come to pass is unpredictable! It is Chaos, I tell you, Chaos!"

"And there ought to be a law? Remember, comrade, that it is this state of unpredictability which nearly every race endures for all of its life-span. It is in this state that we began, and we are unusual in surviving it. We very nearly died of boredom; would that have been more desirable?"

"Don't lecture me!" the Other replied with uncharacteristic sharpness. "I know as well as you do of the dangers that confronted us. I was the first to consent to your plan. Do not begrudge me the right to complain of some of its consequences; it assists me in adjusting to the inevitable."

Laughter crackled through the distorted space around them. "Nothing is inevitable anymore, dear comrade, nothing! That is the entire point of the experiment!"

"Well, I hope your experiment will produce a cure for smugness, then. I personally shall take great pleasure in restraining you while it is forcibly administered!"

Once again laughter sundered the twisted ether as the One, the disgruntled Other, and the Rest, in various states of mind, plunged onward.

"Nonsense!" Rokur Gepta hissed from the corner of his apartments below the control deck. "He is mine to deal with, and I tell you he shall be sectioned alive before the entire crew—yours included, Admiral Shanga—as an example!"

It was the first time the fighter commander had ever seen the sorcerer pace nervously. The time was growing near for the resolution of a number of crises, and the Renatasian had a suspicion that Gepta, too, feared he would be robbed of his victory by a trigger-happy fleet commodore.

Carrying disrespect to new heights because he felt the effect was necessary, Shanga flopped into the sorcerer's huge chair. "Gepta, you old charlatan, you know better than that, and if you don't, I'll tell you now. Keep Bern Nuladeg in the brig, if you wish, until we get to the ThonBoka. He could use the rest, and it'll keep him out of trouble. Not to mention saving your well-concealed face. But execute him, and I'm through with you. I'll take my squadron and—"

"You'll do what you are told!" Gepta made a threatening magical gesture.

Shanga laughed. "Save your parlor tricks, old man! We stopped doing what we were told when your precious Centrality destroyed anything we had to lose by disobeying. Twenty-three loose cannon, Gepta, and they're all pointed at you unless you—"

"Silence! I have no further need for you, Klyn Shanga. You have foolishly told me where Lando Calrissian might be found. We will soon be there, and he is trapped by the fleet, cannot get away from the justice I shall mete out. You serve no purpose. You are dispensable!"

Shanga obtained another cigar from inside his suit, lit it, and spat out a flake of tobacco onto the carpeted floor.

"Yeah? Well, I spent a little time with your pet professor today. You'll recall you instructed him to be free and easy with information bearing on combat operations in the nebula? What he had to say about the guff relayed this morning from the fleet was very interesting. Very interesting, indeed."

Gepta, his back turned to the squadron commander, spoke to the wall. "And what was that?"

"Ask your own people if you don't believe me. We're up against it, Gepta. There are something like a *billion* oswaft in that sack, every one of them as dangerous as a fighter ship. Something about folks like us being electrochemical in nature, our nervous systems, anyway. Well, the oswaft are what your boy is calling 'organoelectronic.' I don't know exactly everything that implies, but they can think and act and maneuver a lot faster than we can. What's more, a flock of them destroyed the *Courteous.* Nobody knows how."

Gepta whirled on Shanga. "What has this to do with disposition of *your* group, *Admiral*?" The way the sorcerer pronounced his title may have been the most sarcastic thing that Shanga had ever heard. With difficulty he shrugged off the implied threat, returned to calculated insult.

"So you think you're going to get anywhere with the clumsy children you've got manning this ship? I told you, Gepta, they're amateurs, and they're so scared at balling things up, they'll ball them up anyway! I think what Bern Nuladeg tried this morning ought to demonstrate pretty well how frightened we are, of you, or of anything else. You need us, you pretentious idiot, and you're going to lose this operation without us. You may have already. Have you heard from the fleet?"

There was a long, long silence while Rokur Gepta gained control of himself. No one, not for perhaps twenty thousand years, had spoken to him in such a manner and lived—or even died a quick and merciful death. In fact some of them had lasted, under one instrument of both torture and regeneration or another, for *centuries*. Klyn Shanga might be one such, after this was over.

Very well, then, the sorcerer reasoned, it should not matter what immediate disposition he made of Shanga or his underlings. They would serve their purpose in the coming conflict, and any who survived . . . But he had one more source of information to consult. He strode rapidly to the chair that Shanga occupied, ignored the man, and pressed a button. "Send me the *Ottdefa* Osuno Whett immediately."

Not three minutes later, the compartment door whisked aside, and the anthropologist stepped in. The tall, emaciated professor took in what was to be seen, sensed conflict momentarily postponed, and vowed to himself to get out of the way as soon as he could manage it.

"You have been following the information from the fleet?" the sorcerer asked without preliminaries.

"Of course, sir, I—"

"What do they tell you of the capabilities of the oswaft?"

Shanga grinned, but kept his silence.

"Well, sir, it is a confirmation of my earlier studies. In a cellular sense, these beings seem to exist on a sort of solid-state level, something like primitive electronics. This accounts for their communications abilities and—"

"How is this known? Is it merely surmise, or are there data?"

The anthropologist's astonishment grew every time Gepta snapped at him. Along with his fear. "Sir, a number of vessels did a full-range scan at the moment the creatures were destroyed. Most of them were vaporized when the *Courteous* went up. In fact, it's possible that not one of them was injured by fire from the fleet. They simply miscalculated the destructive radius of an exploding cruiser. The *Courteous* did open fire, but there wasn't any time to—"

The sorcerer raised a hand and the scientist halted. "By what means did the oswaft destroy the cruiser *Courteous*, Ottdefa? And how vulnerable do you suppose they are to the navy's weapons?"

Whett hesitated before he began again. "Sir, as difficult as it may be to believe, it appears that simple microwaves were the method, but at incredible power levels. This is consistent with their ability to hypertravel, since it, too, is an energy-intensive phenomenon. There is also the fact to consider that the *Courteous* was unshielded—I believe the circumstances are referred to as 'garrison discipline'? Shielded, I believe a ship would be quite safe. To answer your second question, there is no reason to believe that the oswaft would be any more impervious to disintegrator beams, tractor-pressor beams, disruptors, and the like, than any other living thing."

The sorcerer stood deep in thought, one hand where

his chin should have been under his wrappings. Shanga sat, apparently relaxed and smoking his cigar, while Whett stood nearly at attention.

"One final question, *Ottdefa*: how many oswaft are there?"

"Sir, there is no direct way of knowing. Estimates range from several hundred million to a few billion."

Shanga laughed. "Since when do the words 'few' and 'billion' belong in the same sentence. Gepta, they could whittle down the fleet by sheer attrition, and—"

"Silence," the sorcerer said with unusual gentleness, "I must think. *Ottdefa*, I will speak with you later, thank you for your report." The door whooshed open and closed behind the grateful anthropologist.

Then Gepta addressed Shanga. "Admiral, you are no friend of mine, and, after this operation, will never again be an ally. But you have spoken the truth to me, and I am compelled to recognize it. Very well, we shall do as you have suggested. Your man—what was his name?— will remain confined until we reach the nebula, where-upon he will revert to your command. I trust you and your squadron will serve me as you have implicitly prom-ised."

The fighter pilot rose wearily and stubbed out his cigar. Rearranging his newly recovered blaster on his leg more comfortably, he walked toward the door, turned back to the sorcerer at the last moment.

"I haven't any reason to want to send you flowers, either, old man, but we've got a common enemy. We'll stick with you until that's taken care of. Talk to you later." He stepped through the door and was gone.

Scarcely noticing the man had left this time, Rokur Gepta paced awhile more, then, with a more determined stride than before, turned to his chair. He seated himself and activated several cameras. He pushed a button. "For immediate recording and beamcast to the Centrality fleet," he directed unseen technicians:

"Upon the unanswerable authority of the Central Administrator, the Council, and the People of the Centrality, I order you to cease all combat operations upon receipt of this transmission and to return to your positions on the original blockade perimeter.

"Evasion or failure, on the part of any officer, at *any* level, to comply swiftly with this direct order will be punishable by summary revocation of all rank and privileges, judiciary and ceremonial impoverishment and sale into bondage of all family members within five degrees of consanguinity, and for the perpetrator himself, slow mutilation and death upon public display.

"I, Rokur Gepta, Sorcerer of Tund, command it."

The camera lights went out.

Gepta sat back in his chair, feeling much better. This would buy them all some time, and resolve part of the conflict between Klyn Shanga and himself. Odd, he hadn't had a real adversary to stand up to him for thousands of years. No one dared oppose his ruthless exercise of power. Everywhere he went, people in their masses, and as individuals, feared, hated, and served him.

Except for Lando Calrissian.

And now, possibly even worse than the itinerant gambler—because the affront seemed deliberately calculated—there was Klyn Shanga.

The most peculiar aspect of it was that, somehow, it felt good.

TWELVE

T̲HE *OTTDEFA* O̲SUNO W̲HETT R̲EFLECTED.

Shuddering in the relative security of his assigned quarters in officer's country, he considered himself extremely lucky just to be alive that morning. He'd seen others broken, figuratively and literally, at the malignant whim of Rokur Gepta, individuals guilty of nothing more than reporting a purely mechanical failure or bringing him information he didn't want to assimilate. To be trapped in the middle of a dispute between the evil sorcerer and his reluctant—and no doubt soon-to-be *former*—partner, that barbarian Shanga...

He crossed the cramped living-sleeping space allotted him, noting that he'd forgotten to fold the cot into the wall in his earlier haste to answer Gepta's summons. So—he was still accustomed to depending on a servant after all this time. It was a weakness to make note of and correct.

The gray military wallcoat of the compartment still oppressed him, despite the decorations—ceremonial masks, garish shields, primitive hand-powered weapons—he'd hung up here and there. He'd have to see what else he carried in his luggage down below in the storage hold. It would brighten the place up and strengthen the official "cover" that allowed him to travel thus encumbered in the first place.

Entering the tiny head, he sloughed off the casual civilian shipsuit he'd been wearing, now soaked through with perspiration and smelling foul. He wasn't on the schedule for a shower at this time of day, and hadn't had time for it when the fixtures had been operational. Thank the Core for the mixture of intelligent species whose differences in personal habits and physical characteristics made individual quarters (at least at his level of rank) a necessity rather than a luxury even aboard this spartan vessel. At that, it could be worse: he could be quartered with the noncoms or conscriptees. It wouldn't have been unprecedented; his long career had seen him assume many stranger poses. Now all he desired was a refreshing wash, which he attended to at the small sink (set into the shower stall along with the toilet) with its trickle of lukewarm recycled water. An ironic expression greeted him in the mirror above the sink.

Well, he had *survived*, as he had *always* survived. All it had required was layer upon layer of carefully prepared deception. It was the sole art to which he could truly lay claim, the only way he could expect to get out of *this* mess with his skin intact.

That accursed robot: *it* had been responsible for all his troubles in recent years. Gepta and Shanga were headed toward the ThonBoka nebula—from Tund, on the outskirts of one side of civilization, to the Starcave, on the fringes of the other side—for nothing more than revenge. Perhaps he, himself, the *soi-disant Ottdefa* Osuno Whett, would be enjoying a little vengeance, too, when the *Wennis* finally arrived at its destination.

He splashed water on his thin, elongated face, his neck

and bony chest, ran a laser over his stubble, and remembered.

He'd been younger then, of course, and his appearance considerably different. Afterward, he'd had four centimeters of bonemer grafted into each tibia, fibula, and femur to increase his height, proportionate amounts added to his arms as well, and an extra vertebra interleaved in his spine. It was painful, and it had taken several months just to accustom himself to the new leverages, the new bodily rhythms the surgery imposed. He was *still* learning, and, in the meantime, gave an unnaturally awkward and gangling impression. This he welcomed, as it added to his disguise. He'd also lost some forty kilograms—amazing how much that alone had rendered him unrecognizable. The hair had whitened of its own accord, as whose wouldn't in the knowledge that something of the order of a billion individuals wanted to see him painfully dead, and were willing to do something positive about it. He'd left the hair alone, changing only its style. It, too, served his purpose, which amounted simply to staying alive in a murderous business. He'd already outlived the average life-expectancy in his profession by over thirty years.

The tap water shut itself off. He dried himself vigorously with the only towel he'd be permitted on the voyage, picked up the soiled shipsuit from where he'd dropped it, and crossed the cabin to the tiny partitioned alcove where his travel bag hung unfolded. Depositing the old clothes on the closet floor, he got out another set, dressed himself carefully and comfortably, then made another withdrawl from his bag, went to the unfolded bunk with a small electronic device clutched almost desperately in his knobbly fingers.

He lay down, placed the mechanism beside him, drew

a small cable from it, and fastened the eye-mask on its free end over his face. His hand hovered over a large green button on the side of the black plastic case.

Then he paused in thought once more.

The Renatasia had been a lovely system.

He recalled it vividly: eight plump planets and a cheerful medium-size yellow star set a surprising number of parsecs outside the then-current margins of the million-system Empire. Apparently they'd been human-colonized in some dim spacefaring prehistory, although no records of the event survived, either there or in "civilized" reaches. For the Central Administrator a million systems, of course, were not enough. A billion wouldn't be. Thus Renatasia must be brought under the kindly influence of the Centrality.

Renatasia III and IV were the jewels in their cozy and conveniently isolated diadem. From space they appeared warm, lush, green and inhabited by a people who used steel, titanium, and simple organoplastics, were capable of wringing useful amounts of energy from the core of the atom, and who had not only reached but profitably colonized every one of the remaining six bodies in their system, from freeze-dried outermost, to charcoal flambéed innermost—albeit under domes and in burrows, rather than through the total climatic transformation that even the Empire often found too expensive to pursue.

They had not quite reinvented faster-than-light spacedrives, although they were fiddling with its theoretical underpinnings. Nor had they yet made the basic discoveries that would inevitably lead them to such mechanisms as deflector shields, tractor-pressor beams, disruptors, and disintegrators—a fact for which the Centrality navy was later to be rather embarrassedly grateful. For they could also fight, it developed, like the very devil. They'd been doing it for millennia.

Mathilde was the capital city of a nation-state of the same name, located on the second largest continent of Renatasia III. Reception of the system's crude, flat, electronic sound-and-picture transmissions revealed that her citizens spoke a much-corrupted version of the commonest language of the Centrality—this was to serve as justification for the intervention that came later—and were the most prosperous and technologically advanced people in the system, their offworld colonies the most numerous and successful.

The nation-state of Mathilde, along with others like it, was located in the north temperate zone, and divided its activities about equally between agriculture and manufacturing. Just like every other polity in the system, it had forgotten its long-past origins elsewhere in the galaxy. Mathildean writers and scholars speculated about what future explorers would discover among the stars, and whether there was intelligent life in outer space.

A severely damaged civilian star-freighter had first happened upon the Renatasia System by accident. Once it had limped back to port for repairs, her captain had dutifully reported the system's existence to the government. No contact had been made by the freighter, which made things very much easier for the intelligence operative assigned the task of establishing official communications. The *Ottdefa* Osuno Whett.

His academic credentials had always been the perfect cover for a Centrality spy. Where can an anthropologist *not* go and poke his long, thin nose into the most intimate and personal details of a culture?

Before leaving, his superiors had equipped him, more or less against his better judgment, with an assistant, a rather odd little droid of obviously alien manufacture who said his name was Vuffi Raa and that, owing to a mishap of some sort involving a deep-space pirate attack while he was being shipped in a packing crate, he was unable to remember his place of origin or the species who had built him. Whett was scientist enough—and a genuine anthropologist—to be frustrated by the lack of information. Centrality Intelligence was even less helpful. They simply told him to stop asking stupid questions and get on with his assignment. He got on.

Vuffi Raa did prove to be useful in many ways. He was a superb personal valet, had a capacious memory, an astute intelligence with an easy grasp for every cultural nuance. He was utterly obedient—except that Whett couldn't get the little droid to call him master.

Actually, that turned out all to the good. Before landing their small, unarmed entry vessel on the front lawn of the Mathildean chief executive's official residence, among bands and fanfares and uncounted cocked and loaded weapons, Vuffi Raa had been instructed to disguise himself as an organic being with sophisticated plastics simulating skin.

It occurred to Whett that perhaps the droid would then resemble his original manufacturers. It was a galaxy-wide assumption that droids tended to be designed in the image of their makers. However, he shelved the speculation; they had other problems at present.

The robot would pose as the leader of the diplomatic expedition, an envoy from a starry federation way out there, ready to welcome the Renatasians into the fold. That was Whett's habitual deception at work. He assumed the role of humble assistant and secretary. This kept him neatly out of a spotlight he felt it would eventually be safer to avoid, knowing Centrality policy toward unclaimed but occupied territory.

The *Ottdefa* Osuno Whett, lying in his tiny cabin aboard the decommissioned cruiser *Wennis*, en route to the

ThonBoka, paused momentarily in his musings and finally pushed the button on the electronic box beside him on the cot. A tide of relaxation funneled into his brain through the bony wave guides of his eye sockets. It was followed by another and another and another, each successively smaller, yet still soothing. To run the device continuously would put him into deep sleep, a condition he must avoid in the event the sorcerer should call on him again. But the waves of rest were almost as good.

He pushed the button again.

More memories came to him, unbidden.

After the initial, inevitable awkwardness of first contact, the Mathildeans, along with everybody in the rest of the system, took Vuffi Raa to their hearts. He addressed international conclaves. He presided over formal banquets. He was photographed with scantily clad media personalities. He was compelled to turn down offers involving the endorsement of consumer products. Even so, small replicas of the five-limbed droid began showing up in stores almost from the beginning, and several sizable fortunes were made for their enterprising creators.

All the while, a short, plump, dark-haired *Ottdefa* Osuno Whett made observations and unobtrusive recordings. Estimates were made and updated concerning the strength of the Renatasian economy, the effectiveness of the system's defenses. It was accepted as a given that invasion would unite the deeply divided civilization. Whett would have preferred to play upon those divisions, in effect to let the system conquer itself, but the navy was beneath such subtleties. Some effort was made by the authorities to limit the pair's access to high-security installations, but they didn't take account of a spy technology centuries ahead of Renatasia's.

As he lay in his cot aboard the *Wennis*, Whett's mind

was upon another day, another place. His hand hovered over the button of the electronic relaxer, just as it had hovered, in the small cabin of their landing vehicle, over a button on the communicator panel. Pushing the button would transmit all the data he had collected and trigger the invasion by the navy.

"Well, robot, the great moment has arrived! This will make history in the Centrality, alter the history of Renatasia forever—"

"It will bring history to an end in this system, sir, not alter it."

Whett was sitting in the passenger's seat. Their machine was stored near the hotel in which they were living, and the excuse had frequently been offered that Vuffi Raa required certain nutrients and gases in order to subsist in the (to him) foreign atmosphere of Renatasia III. There had been some thought of holding the craft and examining it—the military mind is the same the universe over—but it had been vetoed by a Mathildean chief executive very much aware of the visitor's popularity.

"Cold feet, from a droid? Why haven't you said anything about this before?" Whett was annoyed. The creature was spoiling his moment of supreme triumph. Still, there was no specific way he could fault the machine; it spoke the objective truth, was in fact incapable of speaking anything else. History *would* end for Renatasian civilization within a few days of his pressing the button.

"I am a droid, sir, constructed to obey. Your remark seemed inferentially to require a reply, that is all." The robot sat in the pilot's chair, its limbs at rest, its eye glowing dully in the dim light of the concrete parking garage.

"I suggest that you address me as master, robot."

"I'm sorry, sir, I am not programmed to respond in that area."

Savagely, Whett jammed his thumb down on the button. A small amber light glowed to life on the panel; no other sign appeared. The deed was done, could not be called back.

Vuffi Raa's eye dimmed almost to extinction, as if the power to transmit the treacherous information was being drained from his supply.

The next few days were bedlam, exactly as Whett had expected. The navy appeared at the fringes of the system, close enough to be fully detectable by Renatasian defense sensors. They even let the local military lob a few primitive thermonuclear weapons at them to demonstrate the utter futility of resistance. The fleet's shields glowed briefly, restoring energy consumed by the voyage out, and that was that. Almost.

Unfortunately for the Centrality navy and high-technology aggressors everywhere in space and time, invasions cannot be conducted with continent-destroying weapons or from behind shields. Not unless you're willing to obliterate the enemy, and not at all if you're interested in taking what the enemy has: raw materials, agricultural products, certain manufactured goods, and the potential labor of her citizens. While the fleet sat tight and safe in orbit above the eight planets of Renatasia, 93 percent of the first wave of Centrality troopers were savagely massacred by the locals, using chemical bullet projectors, crude high-powered lasers, poison gases, clubs, meat cleavers, and fists. Eighty-seven percent of the second wave died similarly, even though they'd been forewarned, 71 percent of the third, and so on. The Centrality was winning a glorious, disastrously expensive victory. Troopships carrying replacements began showing up at hourly intervals.

Osuno Whett and Vuffi Raa had gone into hiding briefly after they had summoned the fleet. Nevertheless, they were hunted and hounded across the face of the planet. The relentless natives gleefully cut them off again and again from rescue by their uniformed compatriots.

At long last they joined a force, a remnant of the third wave, which helped them get aboard a shuttle and into the safety of a Centrality battlewagon. But not before the ugly, merciless extermination of two-thirds of the Renatasian population was an evil, personally experienced nightmare they would live with—and sleep with—for the rest of their lives.

Whett, in his cabin on the *Wennis*, pushed the button again.

Waves of relaxation, but regrettably not of forgetfulness, swept through his tense and tortured body as tears coursed down his face. It was a rare moment: generally he merely hated and feared the remaining Renatasians, having for the most part burnt out his circuitry for shame. He had fled their persistent presence for a long, long time. Nor had he been unhappy when, at long last, his superiors had ordered him to "lose" the robot—both an unwelcome reminder and a dead giveaway to pursuers—to Lando Calrissian in a rigged *sabacc* game.

That had been in the Oseon, and things had not turned out well for either the hopes of the Centrality or for those of Rokur Gepta, who had personally supervised that particular operation.

Now, alone with his real pursuers, his memories, Whett realized that it was more than revenge he needed to accomplish in the ThonBoka. He had to see that robot destroyed. It was a dangerous link, in more ways than one, to an even more dangerous past. And he had to see an end, as well, to Captain Lando Calrissian, who could connect his new appearance, adopted before the game, with the robot.

Very well, then: Gepta sought to destroy Calrissian; Shanga sought to destroy Vuffi Raa (because he didn't know the real mastermind was a "harmless" academic he had seen nearly every day); that academic must now seek to destroy them both, gambler and droid.

Still he wondered, after all this time: where *had* that accursed robot come from, anyway?

THIRTEEN

THAT ACCURSED ROBOT SCRATCHED HIS HEAD.

"Politics, saved our lives, Master? I'm not altogether sure I understand."

In reality, the gesture was more a matter of flicking a delicate tentacle tip around the bezel that retained the faceted red lens of his eye, mounted on the upper surface of his headless pentacular "torso." But its meaning was clear; he had picked it up from long association with human beings. As usual, certain aspects of that association puzzled him.

"Well, I'm only guessing, mind you, but a massive operation such as that Edge-blasted blockade out there, especially when it's being carried out in secret, presents a lot of opportunities to people envious of the boys on top." Lando pried up his cigar from where he'd secured it to the edge of the bench top, drew deeply on it, expelled the smoke, and squashed it firmly once again, sideways, into the wad of chewing gum that, in the absence of gravity, held it where it wouldn't float away.

"Do you want this end-wrench, Vuffi, or the adjustable spanner?"

The robot glanced back at his master, squatting on the

deck plates with one leg thrust under the bench for leverage and security, much like the cigar. Lando leaned on a tool chest, assisting. They'd lifted a repair port and the robot peered now into a complex maze of working and semiworking parts.

"Adjustable, Master. This is a section I rigged after we beefed up the shields in the Oseon. All we had in stock were replacements from the Ringneldia, and everything in *that* system is standardized around the diameter of some native bean or other."

It wasn't just the sudden pullback of the murderous Centrality fleet that bothered Vuffi Raa, although it had left thousands of dead oswaft in its wake. While genuinely ignorant, or at least amnesiac, about his own origins, he could infer certain facts about his makers and their culture, and the trouble was, several of the facts in question were contradictory. And current events were bringing him swiftly to a personal crisis involving those contradictions. It was not a situation that any intelligence—even that of a Class Two droid—finds comfortable.

He detached one of his sinuous manipulators, directing it remotely to thread its way into the starboard reactant-impeller units, deep in the bowels of the *Millennium Falcon*. Nothing was actually *wrong* with the system, but had it been a hair more sluggish, they would have been fried by the *Courteous* instead of cheating their way through hyperspace. It didn't pay to tolerate the slightest malfunction, not when they were the only spaceship the ThonBoka had to put up against the Centrality fleet. Those devices not only fed the engines, which was fairly important in itself, but the deflector shields as well. Vuffi Raa and Lando needed every fractional advantage if they weren't going to sell their lives cheaply.

"For example," the gambler continued, craning his

neck to see what the robot was doing beneath the floor, "there'll be one group which will loudly—and correctly—proclaim that this undeclared war against the oswaft constitutes genocide, although they wouldn't hesitate if they'd thought of it first themselves. Then there'll be a gang of middle-of-the-roaders who could do it better or cheaper. Finally, there'll be the ones who regard the action as too gentle and indecisive. They'll want the fleet to sit back and toss in a few planet-wreckers, and *they're* probably the ones we owe for this hiatus."

A little cynical, Vuffi Raa thought before replying. "But Master, there aren't any planets here to wreck, thank the Core."

"Thank three little blue suns out there that went kablooie for that. You're right, although planet-wreckers could make things pretty uncomfortable for our friends the oswaft—not to mention our tender selves. And besides, in interstellar power politics, it's gestures and appearances that count, not actual results. I've long suspected that's why civilizations rise and fall. Especially fall. Try adjusting that vernier, will you? I thought I heard the field blades wobble a little when you nudged it before." He unstuck his cigar again and took a puff.

Another tentacle clicked at Vuffi Raa's "shoulder" and drifted away to check the readings on the control panels forward. It was possible, the droid thought, that the problem was simply an instrument failure, and it would be stupid to repair something that was already in perfect working order.

Each of the robot's five tentacles, usually tapering smoothly to a rounded tip, could also blossom at the end into a small five-fingered hand. In the center of each rested a miniature replica of the large red eye atop his body; he would see what his tentacles saw. This, and the ability to send his limbs off on various errands, caused him to wonder about his creators.

They were hardly stupid; still, there were counter-indications. Here he was, preparing his master's ship for a battle in which he, himself, dare not participate directly. Early in life, he had experimented: attempting combat, in contravention of his deepest-laid programming, had sent him into a coma that lasted nearly a month. He was extremely clever; he could run and hide; physically he was very tough; he could ally himself with individuals like Lando, *quite* capable of the defensive violence necessary to protect themselves and their mechanical partner, Vuffi Raa. But he, himself, simply could not harm another thinking being, whether organically evolved or artificially constructed.

It just didn't make sense. Vuffi Raa took a certain pride in the fact that he was a highly valuable machine, more so, strictly speaking, than the starship he was servicing. Simply as a market consideration, he had a duty to protect his life; anyone attempting to take it demonstrated, by that very act, that they were less valuable, at least in any moral sense that made sense.

Separating a third tentacle from his body, Vuffi Raa dispatched it to check the readiness of the ship's weapons systems, particularly the quad-guns of which Lando was so fond. The *Millennium Falcon* had always fairly bristled with armament, yet, with only two crew-beings to man her, and one of them a pacifist at that, they'd always meant to tie the weapons together cybernetically somehow. In this brief interlude between confrontations with the fleet, they'd scarcely more than begun the task.

His inhibitions could be stretched, Vuffi Raa had discovered. Knowing full well, for example, that the preparations furthered violent activity, he could nevertheless perform them. Moreover, he could fly the *Falcon* for

Lando, maneuvering properly to assure his destruction of the enemy.

How very peculiar, thought the robot. Who made me this way, and what did they intend by it?

"What in the name of the Edge, the Core, and everything in between are they *waiting* for out there?"

Lando fidgeted at the table as Vuffi Raa watched him disassemble and clean his tiny five-shot stingbeam as a final, albeit somewhat silly, preparation for the coming battle. They were in the passenger lounge. The deckplate gravity was set at full normal, and that, thought the robot, was a bad sign. His master liked free-fall best for thinking.

"*For somebody else to get here,*" a tinny, electronically relayed voice answered. It was Lehesu, visible in a monitor screen the robot had installed. In reality, the great being hovered outside in the void not far from the *Falcon*. Given his size, and Lando's environmental requirements, this was the closest the three could come to normal face-to-face conversation.

"What?"

Lando stopped what he was doing with a jolt, one hand poised on the cleaning brush, elbow in the air, shoulders suddenly hunched as if someone had punched him in the stomach. He rose. Slowly he turned, step by step he approached the monitor until his nose nearly rested on the screen. At his side, the half-cleaned weapon dripped solvent on the deck plates.

"*Who*—" he demanded of the manta creature, "—and how the deuce do *you* know?" Some sort of fire flickered in the gambler's eyes, but even Vuffi Raa, long acquainted with the man's moods, couldn't guess what it signified now.

"*Why, Lando, somebody named Wennis,*" Lehesu answered in a tone of injured innocence. He'd come a long way, learning to interpret human vocal inflections and the images of facial expressions he received directly in his brain from the ship's transmitter. He was disturbed now because his friend looked and sounded angry with him.

"As to how I know: it's practically the only thing they're talking about out there, can't you hear them? Something's going to happen when Wennis gets here, something big. Somebody else named Scuttlebutt has it that—"

"Oh my aching field density equalizers!" As the robot watched, his master's expression changed, like the face on a *sabacc* card, from puzzled to exasperated to delighted. The gambler crossed the room again in two strides, threw himself into a recliner, dug around in his shipsuit pockets and extracted a cigar.

"No, Lehesu, I *can't* hear them, remember? And even if I could—well, Vuffi Raa can 'hear' radio signals, but the military uses codes that are intended to preclude eavesdropping."

He lit the cigar, heedless of the flammable fluid all over his hands.

"Dear me!" cried the oswaft in real distress, *"have I been doing something unethical? I shall cease immed—"*

Lando sat up abruptly, pointing his cigar at the monitor like a weapon. "You'll do nothing of the sort—you *can't* do anything unethical to those goons, it's philosophically impossible! Here I've been getting ready to die bravely, and now, casually, you've given us all a chance to survive! By gadfrey, Vuffi Raa, old corkscrew, let's break out a bottle of—*OWWWWCH!*"

Lando's hands glowed a flickering blue as he leaped up from the recliner and began running around the room. Without hesitation, Vuffi Raa thrust out a tentacle and tripped him; he flopped on the deck, yelling, while the robot tossed a jacket that had been hanging on the back of the lounger over the gambler's hands, and wrapped it tight. The fire was out.

"*What's the matter over there?*" the monitor demanded. "*Are you all right?*"

"I will be, once I learn not to play with fire," Lando answered as he sat up. He winced as Vuffi Raa unwrapped the jacket. His hands were tender, but not badly burned. The droid was gone a moment, returned with a sprayer of plaskin and coated Lando's hands until they were shiny with it.

The gambler flexed his fingers with satisfaction. "Pretty close, old fire extinguisher. I'd have had to pick a new profession if it weren't for your quick thinking. And if it weren't for this stuff—" With freshly dried digits, he examined the first-aid spray, then his brow furrowed in thought. He helped Vuffi Raa tidy up the gun-cleaning mess while explaining to the oswaft what had happened, but his voice had an absent quality the robot recognized as the sign of an idea under incubation.

Finally, stubbornly, he relit the cigar he'd flung across the room, sat back in the recliner, and was silent for a solid hour. Vuffi Raa played a few hands of radio *sabacc* with Lehesu, and let the gambler think. He was fresh out of ideas himself, and, like his master, had been resigned to dying at as high a cost to their assailants as possible.

An odd thing, violence, he pondered, watching the computer change a Commander of Sabres in his "hand" to an Ace of Flasks. He'd inflicted violence on Lando in order to save him from a nasty burn, and hadn't felt a qualm down in his programming. Yet, had some third person tried to harm Lando, the robot would have been helpless to remove the threat. Definitely a glitch there.

It bothered him.

"The *Wennis* is a ship, Lehesu, like the *Falcon* here," Lando said an hour later over a steaming plate from the food-fixer.

"So Vuffi Raa tells me. It's a difficult concept to grasp."

"Well, grasp this: it's the personal yacht of Rokur Gepta, Sorcerer of Tund. We've run into that fellow twice before, and not nicely either time. Now that I know he's involved, this whole blockade makes sense. The truce'll be over when he gets here."

The gambler suppressed a shudder, remembering previous confrontations. Once, in the Oseon, the sorcerer had used a device to stimulate every unpleasant memory Lando had, then recycle them, over and over, until he nearly went mad. It had been interference from Klyn Shanga, intent on destroying Vuffi Raa, that had accidentally saved him. They'd rescued Shanga from the wreck of his small fighter afterward and turned him over to the authorities in another system. He wondered where the man was now.

"Well, in any case, I think I've got an idea. You know, in order to win a war it isn't really necessary to defeat your enemy, just make the fight so expensive he'll give up and go away."

"I wouldn't know," the oswaft answered, *"but what you say makes sense."*

"Sure. As I explained to Vuffi Raa, this blockade's bound to have some opposition, possibly in the Centrality Council. It's already expensive, we merely have to make it more so."

"How can we do that? We have no weapons, and the fleet, with its shields up, is no longer vulnerable to our voices, as was the Courteous. *It has occurred to me that*

*it was a good thing I was in a weakened condition when
I met you, otherwise I might have destroyed you in the
same manner."*

The gambler waved a negligent hand at the monitor.
"There was only one of you, whereas I'm told there were
a thousand oswaft in the party that met the *Courteous*.
Never mind that, we're going to let the fleet destroy
itself."

"How?" Both Vuffi Raa and Lehesu spoke this time.

"I have some questions to ask you first: it's really true
you can understand interfleet communications?"

*"Yes, Lando, so could any of my people, given a few
moments' thought."*

"Hmmm . . . All right, what about this synthesizing
business. Can you make *any* substance I ask you to?"

*"As long as it's relatively simple and there are raw
materials to hand, as it were."*

"And the nebula: your elders tell me that there isn't
any food there for you, that it was all 'grazed' out, long
ago. Yet there are raw materials . . ."

"Yes, Lando, where is all of this leading?"

"Out of a mess. One more thing: how long do you
have to rest between hyperjumps, and how accurately
can you predict where you'll break out?"

"Lando," the oswaft said in exasperation, *"I think I see
where you're going with this. You want us to make bombs
or something and plant them on the fleet's vessels. In the
first place, from what Vuffi Raa has told me of weaponry,
bombs aren't all that simple. In the second—"*

"No, no. Nothing to do with bombs at all, and besides,
those ships'll be coming in here shielded to a fare-thee-
well. And in the second, I said we'll let them destroy
themselves, didn't I? I have a plan to make the war
expensive, that's all."

He hunched over the monitor, conspiratorially. Vuffi

Raa leaned toward him, consumed by curiosity. Lando was clearly enjoying this part, and the robot wasn't sure that made him happy.

"Now here's what we'll do..."

FOURTEEN

"*Gentlemen, man your fighters!*"

Klyn Shanga gazed across the cavernous cluttered hangar deck inside the *Wennis* as his squadron climbed into their tiny spacecraft. Even good old Bern was there, snaking up the ladder into his cockpit. He'd served his sentence in durance vile. Gepta had, surprisingly enough, been as good as his word about that.

It worried Shanga. He wondered what the old trickster had up his long gray sleeve. Keeping promises wasn't an expected part of the magician's repertoire, and the fighter commander felt it bode evil.

The noise was deafening as impellers whined, refueling lines were trucked away, commands shouted here and there. There was a constant steady rumble of eager machinery. In a few moments the hangar crew would clear the deck, all inner doors would be sealed, and the huge belly doors of the cruiser would cycle open, giving the Renatasians access to open space.

"This is the confrontation we've been waiting a decade for," Shanga had told his men, all twenty-three of them, lined up at a ragged, ill-disciplined attention in their shabby, mismatched uniforms. They represented a dozen old-style nation-states, most of which no longer existed. They flew craft purchased, borrowed, leased, and stolen from as many Centrality systems, the ships equally threadbare. In common the flyers shared only a thirst for revenge.

"The Butcher awaits us out there," Shanga had said, pointing vaguely toward the hangar doors overhead. Artificial gravity in the hangar had been reoriented to allow easier servicing and launching of the squadron. "He's laughing at us, you know. His very existence, ten years after his crimes, is a mockery of justice. Well, we will silence that laughter, bring justice back to the universe!"

There was no cheering. Some of the Centrality crew members working on the Renatasian squadron had looked up momentarily, impressed more at Shanga's vehemence than at any eloquence he might have possessed. To individuals in a hierarchy such as they served, strong feelings openly expressed were a threat to survival, the highest virtues moderation, compromise, a deaf ear and a blind eye to injustice.

There was nodding among the twenty-three at Shanga's words, acceptance, a grim agreement, a pact. They looked at their commander and at one another, realizing that it might be for the last time.

"And afterward?" Bern Nuladeg lounged against the outstretched wing of one fighter at the end of the line of men, chewing an unlit cigar. "What'll we do then?"

"Afterward, we'll . . ." Shanga tapered off. He hadn't planned for there to *be* any afterward. There were a billion or more oswaft out there, of uncertain capability, allied with the unspeakable Vuffi Raa. The chances any Renatasian would survive the next few hours were slight. Moreover, their safety afterward, in Gepta's hands, was questionable. The sorcerer would be completely unpredictable once he'd won his victory. There'd be nothing to come back to, not in a Centrality fleet commanded from the *Wennis*.

Shanga shook his head as if to clear it of useless speculations. "Afterward you're on your own. Rendezvous with whatever ship will pick you up. Get home the best way you can—if you want to go home. For the time being, my friends, we live only for justice, only for revenge."

There was muttering, but it was in resigned agreement with what their commander had said. If there was any future, let it come on its own terms, its very arrival a surprise.

They boarded their fighting vessels.

Shanga strapped himself into his pilot's couch, made sure the canopy seals were good, that all mobile service implements had been properly detached and the access ports dogged down. He watched the hangarmen file out through various oval doorways in an unpanicky haste as the big red lights came on to signal the beginning of the cycling process. In effect, the hanger now became a huge airlock; he knew from long experience that, despite the best efforts to filter and scrub the salvaged air, the rest of the ship, from control deck through officer's country down to the scuppers, would smell of aerospace volatiles for several hours.

It was a good smell, he thought to himself, an agreeable one to die with in your lungs if you couldn't arrange for soft grass and evergreen boughs.

He flipped switches and the whining of his engines raised in pitch, the cockpit vibration skipped a beat and settled in a newer discordance with the other machine noises. Adrenaline was rushing into his bloodstream. By the Core, he was a *warrior*. Say what you like about that, you simpering peace-dogs, he was born and bred to *fight*!

The hangar doors above him ponderously ground aside.

"*Five and Eighteen out*!" a voice said in his helmet. Two fighters filled the hangar with exhaust mist as they lifted and roared out into space. The vapor cleared quickly. "*Fourteen and Nine out!*" "*Six and Seventeen!*"

In pairs his men took to the void, as eager for a fight as he was. His onboard computer held a three-dimensional map of the ThonBoka with probable locations for the *Millennium Falcon* marked therein. It was known that there were three small blue-white stars, and some artificial structure, much larger than the freighter, at their center. That would be the prime area for the search.

The "destroy" part would follow immediately.

"*Two and Twenty-one*!" another voice shouted, then Shanga himself felt a severe jolt and the blood stress of acceleration as the hangar catapult-pressor latched onto his command ship and flung it into space among his men. Others continued to pour from the *Wennis* in the same manner, in an order tactically determined by the motley mixture of ship types and models available to them. "*Nineteen and Four!*"

They assumed a complicated formation, hovering until all of the squadron was free of the hangar bay. In the center of the group lay Pinnace Number Five, the very auxiliary Bern Nuladeg had been apprehended trying to steal. Her after section glowed and pulsed with pent-up energy. They were still a relatively long way from the nebula, at least where the small fighters' capabilities were concerned. Even once they got there, it was six light-years to the center—approximately twenty-five times their own maximum flying range.

The pinnace, capable of faster-than-light travel, had been fitted with a tractor field. Unmanned, controlled remotely by Klyn Shanga, it would tow them into the heat of battle, returning parsimoniously on its own to the *Wennis*. He and his best computer doctor had checked the lend-lease auxiliary carefully from bow to stern for ugly practical jokes and delayed-action booby traps. He just couldn't bring himself to trust Rokur Gepta's generosity.

That worthy had been unavailable at debarkation time, apparently gone off to meditate or something. Just as well: his orders to release the Renatasian squadron had been there in his place. To the Edge with the sorcerer, Shanga thought. With any luck at all, they'd never see each other again.

He tapped the keyboard, checking the positions of his tiny fleet clustered about the pinnace. "This is Zero Leader," he announced. "Eleven, tighten up a little on Twelve—that's it. Twenty-two, you're idling a little ragged, aren't you? What's your toroid temperature?"

The fusion-powered fighters would conserve reaction mass, relying on the cruiser's auxiliary to do the work, but they must keep their systems up for instant combat readiness. Belt and suspenders, Shanga thought, belt and suspenders. The old saw was wrong about old, bold pilots, but this was the only way it could be done.

"*Nominal*," Twenty-two replied. He was a young kid from a continent half a world away from Mathilde, Shanga's nation-state. There'd been a time when he'd been supposed to hate that accent. "*I think the trouble's in the telemetry, sir.*"

"Don't call me sir, Twenty-two, and watch that temperature. I want the Butcher just as badly as you do, but charging in there with a malfunctioning ship isn't going to help any of us accomplish that. I don't trust those Centrality maintenance people to clean their own fingernails. You'd better be telling me the truth, son."

"Well, sir—Klyn—maybe I'm a little in the red, but I think this hop will burn out the hot spots."

"All right," Shanga replied grudgingly. "Twenty-three, what the Core's wrong with your life-support? I've got red lights all over the readout!"

"Just lit my cigar, boss. The atmo-analyzer don't like it much." Bern Nuladeg laughed. "Can't get into a dog-fight without I got a stogie in my mouth, I'd bite my danged tongue!"

Shanga grinned inside his helmet, suppressed a chuckle. "Roger, Twenty-three, it's your funeral. All right, men, synch your navi-mods to me. We'll move on the tick. Four, three, two, one—*unh!*"

As a unit, the entire squadron lurched forward, pro-pelled by the pinnace, began accelerating smoothly, and moved off toward the ThonBoka. Now, before the com-ing disorientation of the jump, Shanga and his men had time to look around them.

Ahead, the Starcave looked like a huge eyeball seen in profile. They approached the entrance obliquely to maximize the element of surprise. It was a stupid ritual, Shanga realized; they'd be seen coming anyway. But it was something to begin the program with; it didn't really matter. A huge gray eyeball with no iris, a pupil that twinkled with three tiny, blue-white highlights. Down deep inside that thing was the Enemy. Deep down inside that thing was death.

With a joyous shout of violated natural law, the squad-ron leaped toward it.

W325 was the designation of a very small bathtub-shaped object whose size and power output did not quite earn it the status of an auxiliary vessel. More than any-thing else, it was a rigid, powered spacesuit, used to inspect and repair the hull of the *Wennis* while she was in deep space—but most assuredly *not* under way.

At the moment, *W325* was electromagnetically tied in place well aft of the hull to a boxlike addition to the superstructure supporting the cruiser's main drive tubes. While their fires were momentarily quenched to allow the launching of Klyn Shanga's squadron, they still glowed with waste heat energy. Attached to the underside of *W325* was a decal in the shape of a human being. More correctly, a human being in the shape of a decal.

The *Ottdefa* Osuno Whett, anthropologist and master spy for the Centrality knew he was taking a terrible chance. That was always the case when serving two masters. He owed Rokur Gepta his assistance and advice—and stood to benefit by it to the tune of the destruction of his enemies. To one other, he owed everything, including his life, if need be. His immediate assignment was keeping an eye on the perfidious sorcerer. Gepta was not trusted as naively as he may have thought, gift cruiser or no gift cruiser.

Thus, encased in a slim, flexible spacesuit whose color had been adjusted to match that of *W325*, the anthropologist lay spread, arms and legs stretched wide, as tightly as he could to the undersurface of the little space-faring object while its master was otherwise occupied. Whett's own attention was elsewhere; he watched the readouts in his helmet closely, his curiosity and excitement mounting.

Above, Rokur Gepta cycled out of the small vessel, moved across to the rear surface of the superstructure addition. Whett had already determined, by means of various probes and rays, that the unconventional add-on was composed of hull armor, thicker than most and impenetrable to his devices. He'd suspected something like this and come forearmed. It had not been easy to strew the sorcerer's path with a dozen information-gathering devices, each the size of a single dust mote, but he had done it. Some of them read out in real time. They would be useless in another moment. But some absorbed what they witnessed and would spew it all out in a fraction of a microsecond once Whett was within receiving range again.

Whett waited.

At the rear of the armored compartment, the sorcerer hung. There was no port within sight, no airlock. Whett wondered mightily about that. He did not believe in the reputed powers of the Sorcerers of Tund. He'd seen far too much primitive mumbo jumbo backed up by trickery and hidden technology to be impressed by such claims. He wished that he dared peek out around the hull of *W325* to see what was happening. Instead, he relied on his devices.

Oddly, the real-time machinery gave the impression that Gepta hadn't bothered with a spacesuit. Strange, but not totally unaccountable. No one was quite sure what species Gepta belonged to although he deliberately gave the impression he was human. And there were a people or two that could stand hard vacuum for several minutes—and of course there were the oswaft... There was also the possibility that the sorcerer concealed life-support equipment beneath his robes. It would be like him, and indeed, the lightweight pressure suit the anthropologist wore could be concealed thus.

Whett waited.

As expected, the telltales in his helmet winked off abruptly. Gepta had entered the compartment and was now shielded by what the spy estimated to be at least a meter of incredibly tough state-of-the-art alloy. Slowly he detached himself from the underside of the maintenance vehicle, worked out a few stiff joints, and peered cautiously around the bulge of the craft.

Gepta was gone. There was no sign of him. Nor was there any sign of the means by which he'd entered. One instrument on Whett's helmet panel flickered fitfully in response to radiation leakage. Something hot was going on inside the shielded compartment, but he couldn't tell what. Whatever it was, it was unfamiliar.

He jetted up smoothly to the rear of the compartment and inspected it closely. As he had guessed, there was no airlock, no door of any kind. He rounded the corner and inspected a side, then another and another and another. No sign. He applied sophisticated instruments, highly developed skills. It was a solid box of metal, approximately ten meters on a side, featureless, except...

But that was ridiculous. Precisely in the center of the aftmost surface was a service petcock, opening on a pipeway no more than four centimeters in diameter. He didn't dare lift the cover, but he hung there in free-fall for a dangerously long while pondering, running through a catalog in his head of species and their capabilities.

The Sorcerers of Tund. No investigator—spy or anthropologist—had ever gotten a crack at those mysterious old prunes. He'd regretted Gepta's decision to pick him up in transit, he'd wanted to see Tund, be the first. His employer would have liked that, too.

The Sorcerers of Tund were reputed to have some mighty powers—if you believed in that nonsense—but he couldn't recall any legends about dematerialization or the ability to squeeze through tiny apertures. Magic? Perhaps there was something, after all, to the idea that...

But that was ridiculous.

FIFTEEN

Aboard the *Wennis*, Rokur Gepta prepared himself for battle.

There were mental exercises peculiar to Tund, disciplines of ancient ancestry; weapons to inspect, both personal and aboard the cruiser; personnel to instruct and threaten. Communications had begun flowing from the Centrality fleet. Gepta occupied the bridge, watching, listening, replying. A steady traffic of messengers rushed back and forth between the sorcerer and a hundred points within the ship.

"No," Gepta hissed at the monitor before him, "you will *not* deviate from your designated position, my dear Captain, even to pursue escaping vessels—*especially* not to defend yourself, is my meaning clear, sir? You are a ship of the line. You are expected to perform your duty as specified, never to question orders, to consider yourself and your command expendable in the service of the Centrality.

"We have now spoken for two minutes too long on this subject. Out."

He waved a hand; the disappointed features of the captain of the *Intractable* faded from the screen. It was the third such conversation he'd conducted within the hour, and he was growing weary of it. Only the thought of what lay aft in its armored compartment, the lovely green death, enabled him to remain calm.

"General Order!"

An electronically equipped secretary hurried to his side, a recording device clutched fearfully in hand. "While it should not be necessary," Gepta dictated, "to instruct officers in the line of their duties to the Centrality, some question has arisen as to the advisability of their writing their own orders upon no other discretion than the wish to preserve their ship or their personal interpretation of their purposes in being here.

"To resolve these uncertainties, and as an example for future individualists, the commanding officers of the *Intractable*, the *Upright*, and the *Vainglorious* are hereby stripped of rank, along with their seconds in command. Said command will revert to the third officer in succession, and the six above-mentioned personnel will be placed unprotected in an airlock, which shall be evacuated into empty space.

"By the authority of the Central Administrator, Rokur Gepta, Sorcerer of Tund. Did you get all of that, young man?"

The stenographer, his face grown white, nodded dazedly. "Y-yes, sir."

"Good. Send it out and make sure it's understood that the order is to be carried out immediately. Now run along."

Beneath his headdress windings, Gepta smiled. Aside from his two sessions in the armored compartment aft, this was the best he'd felt all day.

Vuffi Raa sat in the lefthand seat of the control room of the *Millennium Falcon*, setting up problems on the navigational console and cross-playing them through his master's game computer. He had to admit, Lando had been right. His scheme wouldn't win a war, and it might cost a great many lives on both sides, but it would wear the fleet down and encourage Gepta's political opponents to step in and end the blockade. Had he been capable of shaking his head ironically, he would have done so.

He looked out through the segmented viewport forward, where he saw Lehesu hanging peacefully—at least to all appearances. He keyed the com. "I have completed the modeling exercise, friend Lehesu. I believe we have a good chance. Will you not join the others with their preparations?"

The giant creature swam closer to the *Falcon* and peered in at his little robot friend. *"No, Vuffi Raa. I am aware of what I must do, and I am ready. I was curious as to the projections you are undertaking. Will the fleet truly destroy itself if Lando's plan works?"*

The droid raised a tentacle to indicate certainty since he couldn't nod. "Yes, as unbelievable as it may seem. You are an amazing people, my friend, and that's what makes it possible. The *Falcon* is as ready as she'll ever be, although I—"

"You are troubled, Vuffi Raa?" Lehesu could interpret tones of voice even with a mechanical being. *"Please speak to me about it; perhaps that will help."*

Glancing mentally at the timepiece he carried in his circuitry, the robot gave his equivalent of a shrug. "It is like this, Lehesu . . ." He told the oswaft of the conflicts he felt in his programming and that he was beginning to disapprove of those who had imposed it on him. It didn't seem right that he should be compelled to stand by idly— at least what he considered to be idly—while the Centrality exterminated a gentle, admirable people.

"I see," the alien replied at last. *"You know, we are*

in much the same position. I do not know whether I can take a life in my own defense, either. We are not a fighting people, as you so rightly have observed. Perhaps it is time for us to abandon life to make room for a more successful product of evolution."

The robot, not knowing what to say, said nothing.

"Then again, Vuffi Raa, we should go away only if we cannot change. If we can, we are a successful species, are we not?"

Momentarily, Vuffi Raa wished he could smoke a cigar like his master. It seemed to help the human think, and it lent a certain dignity to whatever answer he might give the oswaft. "I do not know, my friend. It seems wrong somehow that the success of a race be measured by its ability to do violence. There are other things in the universe."

The oswaft was no more capable of nodding than the robot. *"Still, one must consider that none of these things are any good to one if one is dead."*

Vuffi Raa chuckled. "You have a point, there, Lehesu, you have a point."

"We are going to be too late!" the Other complained. "I know it!"

"Peace, my old friend," the One replied. "That is not yet a foregone conclusion. There are no foregone conclusions anymore. And even so, it is an experiment. It would not be valid, did we interfere. Any result is a desired result, am I not correct in this?"

They bored through the endless night at a velocity that seemed a crawl to them, although a good many physicists in the Centrality would have been interested to know such a velocity was possible. Behind them stretched an endless line, the Rest who had come to witness the results of the One's experiment.

"However," the Other replied, hesitating in his thought if not in his headlong flight, "I have had a disturbing new thought which—"

"That was the purpose of the experiment, was it not?"

"Yes, yes. But I do not believe you are going to be particularly happy with it. You see, it has occurred to me that, despite the unconventional methods by which you created our experimental subject, and despite the obvious anatomical differences..." Here, the Other made a gesture emphasizing the smooth, rounded shape of their kind.

"Yes? Please continue."

"Do not be impatient; this is difficult. I have come to believe we have certain responsibilities toward this entity—specifically that you do—beyond simple scientific inquiry."

There was a long pause as another several parsecs whisked behind them. Nor did the One reply at all. For once his friend had pursued a line of reasoning where he could not easily follow.

"You are its parent."

"What?"

"You brought it into existence. You sent it out into the universe. We—you—cannot blandly let it be destroyed. Such would be reprehensible."

Again the One failed to respond. The light-years rushed by as he plunged himself deep into thought, pondering not only the question of his responsibility, but the more disturbing thought that he had overlooked the issue entirely. Their experimental subject was a thinking being, not to be trifled with as if it were an inanimate object. Apparently complacency had cost him more than progress and the flavor of life, it had interfered badly with his ethical sensibilities.

At last: "I am afraid you are right, my old friend.

Congratulate me, I am a father. And by all means, let us hurry, lest we be too late!"

"It's simple, really," Lando explained for the fifth time with as little hope of success as he'd enjoyed the first four. "You jump into the middle of a pair of ships, do the little trick we've discussed, and jump out. The navy'll do the rest."

The gambler floated in the lotus position in the center of the Cave of the Elders, Sen and Fey on either side of him. Each of the gigantic beings was at least five hundred times larger than he was. He felt like a virus having polite tea with a pair of bacteria.

"But Captainlandocalrissiansir, it is disgusting!" Fey complained. "It is demeaning, beneath the dignity of any—"

"How do you feel about losing your transparency?"

"What do you mean?"

Lando drew on the cigar he'd gotten Vuffi Raa to build a holder for in his suit helmet. There was a slight bulge now in the faceplate, and the air filters had needed overhauling, but at long last he could sit and think properly in hard vacuum.

"Isn't death demeaning, beneath your dignity, disgusting?"

There was the distinct sensation that the younger of the two Elders had blinked with surprise. "Why, I had never thought of it that way before."

Sen had remained silent through this argument. Now he spoke up. "Tell me, Lando, could you perform the physiological equivalent of this act? To excrete bodily wastes in order to—"

"You bet your biffy I could! Look: all that this requires is that you concentrate a certain mix of heavy metals in your systems, hop to the right coordinates, let your pores do their work, and hop out, leaving a sensor-detectable oswaft-shaped outline behind for the boys in gray to shoot at. Play your cards right and, human reaction-time being what it is, they'll shoot each other, instead."

Sen and Fey thought about that. For rather too long a time, Lando thought.

"Listen, you two, you didn't hesitate to offer me all kinds of precious jewels, and you manufacture them in the same—"

"It's not the same at all!" Fey wailed. "Don't you understand that it's different when one—"

"Not from *my* cultural standpoint. On the other hand, most humans I know see a big ethical difference between killing animals for food and killing vegetables—although I've met a photosynthetic sentient or two who might give them an argument. Let's leave it that cultures often have blindnesses about themselves that other cultures see more clearly. Can you do this thing?"

The soft twinkling of precious stones gleamed through the transparent Elders. "Those of us who can, will rendezvous with you at your signal."

The gambler shrugged. "Guess I can't ask for more than that, can I?"

He sensed that Sen was smiling. "No, I suppose you cannot, unless one wishes to emulate the enemy we are about to fight."

As his fighter squadron passed through the mouth of the ThonBoka, Klyn Shanga was fighting a nagging thought. Like a tune that circles through your consciousness all day (whether you like the tune or not—and, more often than not, you don't), he was wondering about the *Ottdefa* Osuno Whett. Why did that son-of-a-mynock seem so familiar? Where had he seen him before?"

"Seventeen, square up a little on the mark. You're lagging, and it's putting a strain on the pinnace."

"Roger, Zero Leader. Executing."

He gave a quick glance at the other computer-generated indicators on his boards and settled back in his acceleration couch again. Where had he met the tall, skinny, white-haired anthropologist before, and why did he have trouble thinking of him as an academic. What should he be? A flunky of some kind. Whett was born to be a subordinate.

But why? He came to the conclusion that it wasn't Whett's appearance he remembered so vividly. The voice, then? A high, whiny, nagging voice it was, full of a high opinion of himself that didn't seem to fit the vague memory Shanga had. It was like the false memories one experiences in dreams: you wake up suddenly (and often with relief) knowing that the thing you remembered never happened at all. But Whett was real.

"Twenty-three to Zero Leader, over."

"Go ahead, Bern."

"Sure. How come we're not maintaining commo silence on this run? I thought we were gonna surprise the little—"

"They know we're coming, and there's only one direction we can come from."

"Kinda like that first raid we made south of Mathilde, after the Betrayal, right?" Nuladeg chuckled at the bloodsoaked memory. It was the only thing they could do. The reminisence wasn't that pleasant, although they'd killed a thousand Centrals that morning, caught them on the ground before they got set up for defense. He remembered the shock he'd felt at the invasion, after all the friendly welcoming they'd done for Vuffi Raa and—

Now why did *that* make him think of Whett again?

"Zero Leader to Twenty-three. Bern, have you seen Gepta's pet anthropologist, Osuno Whett?"

"Can't say as I have. How come?" Shanga could see the other fighter's craft on the opposite side of the formation, its cockpit full of cigar smoke. He wondered how the little man breathed in that atmosphere.

"I don't know, Bern, but there's something nagging me, and it seems to be important."

"Stop chewing on it, then, boss. Sleep it over. It'll come to you if it's important. Core, you could use a little shut-eye, anyways. Sit yourself back, and I'll take the con for a while."

"Thanks a lot, Bern, I appreciate it."

"Just so you don't make a habit of it."

"Roger, Twenty-three, and out."

The *Ottdefa* Osuno Whett looked over some highly peculiar data as he sat in the cramped confines of his hiding place. Outside, the stars appeared motionless through the ports. It was an illusion.

According to the almost microscopic spy devices he'd planted on Gepta with only partial success, the wizard had indeed entered that armored compartment aft of the *Wennis* through a tube scarcely larger than a child's wrist diameter. And somewhere within that tube, according to these readouts, Gepta had ceased to exist, for the dust-mote-sized recorders had drifted in the tube and remained there, recording nothing, until the sorcerer again became himself.

Whatever *that* was.

Whett shifted uncomfortably on his couch, not daring to show a light that might be seen from the outside, not believing the readouts, their displays stopped down to near invisibility. He'd known others in his field—anthropology, not spying—who'd eventually come to believe in the primitive magic they studied, otherwise serious scholars who thought that dancing, after all, at least when performed a certain way by a certain people, could bring rain. Good minds gone to rot from nothing more than overexposure, some malignant form of osmosis. He'd always resisted that, regarded it as a failure both of scientific detachment and personal integrity. Now, he wasn't sure.

All right, the Sorcerers of Tund were supposed to have been capable of all kinds of magic. No one had ever claimed that they were even human; that was a general assumption, and, like all general assumptions, was probably mistaken. Nonetheless . . .

What species was *naturally* capable of the thing his instruments had witnessed? Gepta had returned through the tube, the electronic motes adhering to him again as he, what—materialized? And what was that weird, unknown radiation that, despite armor he now realized was not one but two meters thick, incredibly still leaked out when Gepta had been inside the compartment for a few minutes?

And most of all, what, in the Name of the Core, *was* Rokur Gepta?

SIXTEEN

"*MASTER, WE'VE GOT COMPANY!*"

"All right, Vuffi Raa, I'm coming!"

Lando jumped up from his seat in the lounge where he'd been programming tactics for the oswaft. Out of over a billion of the creatures, less than a thousand had agreed to play his great game of *sabacc*, live or die. He ran around the corridor to the cockpit and flung himself into the righthand seat.

"Where away?"

The robot indicated a tightly strung series of blips on the long-range sensors. "Fighters, Master, the same kind we fought in the Oseon. I make it twenty—no, twenty-five. I don't know what that big thing in the middle is."

The gambler nodded. "I wonder if it isn't the same group. They don't look like a tactical fighter wing, and they're using the same formation they did before. Last time it was a battleship engine." He began throwing switches, bringing the *Falcon*'s defensive armament to full readiness.

"Oh my," Vuffi Raa said in a subdued voice, "the Renatasians. Sometimes I think it would be better just to surrender myself to them. If only they knew the truth."

"Cut it out, sprocket-head! They *know* the truth, it's just too hard to let go of a scapegoat once you've got him by the chin-whiskers. Let's surprise those mynock-smoochers by going out to meet them, what say?"

The robot's tentacles began dancing over the boards. "My sentiments exactly, Master, that's what we came here for in the first place, wasn't it?"

Lando rose, steadying himself against a chair as vibrations washed through the ship. "Quite right, although I wasn't sure we'd sucker the Renatasians in, too. Gepta's overdue. How can he resist having us trapped here in the Starcave?"

"Don't worry, Master, he'll show up."

"Swell." The gambler made haste aft to the tunnel connecting with the quad-gun bubble, reached the swiveling chair and strapped himself in. "Well, old friend, let's go!"

"Yes, Master," the intercom answered. *"Full power coming up!"*

As the *Falcon* rushed to meet the foe, Lando reviewed his plans. The oswaft wouldn't strike the small group of fighters. He'd cranked his ideas through the computer and, from there, directly into their brains. They now knew as much about tactics as he did.

Refocusing on the task at hand, he limbered up, swung the guns up and down, side to side. The chair followed with them, giving him an exhilarating ride that was probably the real reason he liked the weapon so much. He keyed the intertalkie. "Test coming up—and don't call me master."

"Yes, Mas—"

"Got you that time." Using one of the stars for a point of aim, he pressed both thumbs down on the triggers. Bolts of high-intensity energy shot from the guns as they pumped back and forth in their odd pattern, much like the reciprocating machine guns of old. Only now, it was to avoid a backwash of power that would have fused the muzzles of the nonfiring barrels. He fired the guns again, then looked at the repeater screen to see what Vuffi Raa was seeing up ahead.

"One thousand kilometers and closing, Master. That central object is a ship's pinnace. I believe they used it for tow. Shields up at eight-fifty kilometers. They're beginning to cast off the pinnace."

"Hold her steady, little friend, let them make the first pass."

On his screen, Lando could see that the fighters had erected their deflectors, too. Fighter shields were notoriously porous, there just wasn't enough ship—or engine—to support them. That's one thing that made a vessel the size of the *Falcon* so handy.

"Five hundred kilometers, Master."

Now the fighters were visible as tiny dots of light, pseudostars against the starry background of the ThonBoka mouth. Lando brought his guns to bear, swinging to meet the enemies' maneuvers, getting a feel for them. Felt like Klyn Shanga's bunch, all right. Apparently they'd teamed up with the sorcerer and the navy.

Two fighters streaked over the Falcon. Lando poured destructive energy at them, but the pass was too fast for either side to do any damage. They were probably confirming that this was, indeed, the *Millennium Falcon*, Vuffi Raa, a.k.a. the Butcher of Renatasia, first mate.

The robot heeled the ship steeply. *"Two coming up from below!"*

"Let 'em come!" The ship's beefed-up shields would be a surprise. Lando held his fire until the last moment, then pounded into the larger ship of the two. Its shielding lasted all of a millisecond, then there was an explosion and the vessel corkscrewed off, badly damaged.

He swung the guns around, but the second fighter had passed overhead and was gone. One down, he thought, and by Vuffi Raa's estimate, twenty-four to go. "Damage report!"

"Nothing to report, Master. Our shields held fine."

"You do great work. Where'd they go?"

The question was answered as six fighters bored directly for the freighter. Lando sprayed the space in front of them with energy, the ship's lights dimming briefly as he did. They veered sharply, unable to match his fire at that range.

"Master! Bandits straight ahead! Eleven of them!"

"Well, slew the ship! I can't reach them from here! No! Cancel that! I've got trouble enough!"

Four of the original six were back, shooting hard. Lando matched them shot for shot, smoked another, then caught a figher with a direct hit. It blossomed into an enormous ball of tiny sparks and disappeared. But the others didn't give up yet. Even the wounded ship executed a wide, clumsy circle and came back. Lando centered the lead fighter in his crosshairs, thumbed the ignition, and growled.

Another fireball. Another hit on the crippled ship, which wobbled, skidded off, then suddenly exploded. The remaining fighter fought its way around a corner and lunged out of range. It'd be back.

"Clear, now! Turn the ship!"

"Too late, Master, I destroyed two fighters and the other nine broke off."

There was a long, startled pause that nearly cost the two their lives. A single fighter came in at top speed, fired all its retros, dumped its load of lethal energy directly onto the stern tubes, the weakest portion of the shielding. Lando started, more frightened at his inattention than by the fighter. He swung the quad-guns aft, fired and fired until the single fighter vanished in a cloud of smoke.

The pilot of that vessel couldn't have been more surprised than Lando was. "You say you shot down two fighters, old pacifist?" This much was true: there was a pair of small guns, usually ineffective against anything bigger than a rowboat, located on the upper surface of the ship and controllable from the cockpit. Lando had wanted them synchronized, which would effectively quadruple their power, and Vuffi Raa had gotten around to it in the last few days.

Still, there was no reply from the control deck.

"Vuffi Raa, are you all right?"

No answer.

The fighter group had broken off momentarily, licking their wounds, no doubt, and sizing up the *Falcon*. If it was Shanga's people, they were probably surprised to meet *two* columns of fire coming in.

Or were they? Tactically, they'd known Vuffi Raa couldn't shoot back, yet politically (psychologically? sociologically?) he was the most murderous villain in their history. How did they resolve a conflict like that?

"Vuffi Raa, speak to me!"

"Yes, Master. I beg your pardon, and I'll tell you all about it later. No time now—our friends are back!"

This time they came in force. Lando counted seventeen before he got busy, which agreed approximately with the five kills and one probable they'd scored thus far. Lando wasn't taking trophies; it wasn't in him to do it. He simply wanted to know how near the end of the fight they were getting. He wanted a cigar.

This time they gave it all they had, as well. Lando slugged it out, and he could sense the drain on the ship's engines that meant Vuffi Raa was shooting while he steered the ship. Still, the shields were taking a terrific pounding, and yellow lights, to judge from the robot's shouted reports, were showing up like fireflies on the boards.

Then a bright light bloomed where Lando's guns weren't pointed and Vuffi Raa's couldn't be. Standing off, without the benefit of shields, was Lehesu. He turned slowly, majestically, "shouted" at another figher, which turned into a knot of greasy smoke, then disappeared himself, to show up on the other side of the ship.

The fighters broke off at some distance; peace reigned momentarily.

"Lehesu, you old ace! I thought you were with your people!"

"My people are intelligent life everywhere, Captain-master. I saw you needed help, and—"

The gambler frowned. "I wouldn't exactly say we needed help, exactly." Retrieving a cigar from where he'd tucked it in his boot top, he lit it and settled back for a moment.

"I would," Vuffi Raa said. *"Thank you, Lehesu, and thank you for the talk. I seem to have resolved the conflict in my programming."*

Keeping an eye on the indicators for further intruders, Lando asked, "Where are your people, Lehesu; are they waiting to follow my program?"

"No, Captainmaster. Instead, they have followed your example. They have gone to confront the fleet instead of waiting for it."

The entity whom Lando referred to as Sen was grati-fied. Something more than a thousand oswaft swam now behind him, many more than he had counted on, shamed by Captainmasterlandocalrissiansir's valiant example— and possibly his successes against the first wave of the enemy. He directed a thought toward Fey.

"How many would you say we are, old friend?"

"Perhaps as many as a million. The rest have followed another of the human's suggestions: they are concealing themselves in the walls of the Starcave."

A mental shrug. "Well, they may be right, and that may save us from extinction better than doing battle with these monsters. This idea of individual dissent that Lehesu forced upon us may have its uses. Different opinions produce different modes of survival, one or more of which may succeed."

The fleet grew as they approached it.

"I do not know," Fey said. "I believe I would prefer to be playing *sabacc* just now. The notion of being killed—"

"Is faintly refreshing," finished the older of the two Elders. "Lehesu is right: it is better than sitting around becoming stagnant."

"Everyone to his own preferences," Fey answered wryly.

Aboard the *Reluctant*, a gunner's mate finally tore his eyes away from the scope. "A million of 'em! Core save us, there's a million of 'em out there!"

His supervisor hurried over, looked down from the catwalk into the mate's instruments while the mate looked up in fear and wonder at him. "You're wrong, son, the computer's making a new estimate. Make that *two* million."

Sen chuckled to himself as he hopped out of the artificial skin he'd just generated, leaving it behind to confound the enemy. Their sensors would now be registering three million oswaft, and even if they fathomed the trick, they wouldn't know which outline to shoot at.

One chance in three of getting killed, instead of unity.

♦ 160 ♦

You could learn things from *sabacc*. He hopped another hundred meters, paused, and made it one chance in four. Every step his people took this way increased their apparent numbers arithmetically. The real test would come when they reached the fleet and began swimming in its midst.

"Are you ready, old friend?" asked Fey at his side.

"No. Let's go."

Their first leap took them within firing distance of the *Reluctant*. Before she could bring their guns to bear, they were gone. Sen angled his next jump to place him between that vessel and the next in the metallic swarm. He hopped, created a ghost of himself, and hopped again, this time to a safe place where he could watch.

Reluctant belied her name and *fired*! The powerfully huge bolt, a recent Imperial development, sliced through the false oswaft, scoring a deep and crippling hit on her sister vessel, who had fired only slightly behind the other ship. This bolt was a near miss, but it caught an escort fighter and vaporized him instantly. The oswaft outline dissolved and was gone.

Sen jumped again, creating another threatening image of himself. It had much the same effect as the first: the enemy counted on a target to absorb the lethal force of his guns before they struck a Centrality sister vessel. They were wrong, and discovering it too slowly. A million oswaft followed Sen and Fey, repeating the same actions. Space was lit with thousands of fierce, futile bolts. Men died by the hundreds until the trick was finally puzzled out.

By then it was too late. Shouting at the top of his voice, Sen crumpled a pair of fighters, then concentrated his energies on a cruiser. Lando was right: her shields were too dense to have any effect. He stopped shouting at everything but the gnatlike fighters, and hopped and hopped, making sure each time to place himself between two capital ships.

For their part, as they saw the destruction of their own numbers by their own guns, the navy slowed even more, trying to aim its fire so as not to endanger the fleet. This was useless: either there was nothing to shoot at, or the bolt would knife through the observed enemy, blasting a cruiser or a dreadnaught instead.

In fifteen minutes, the Centrality fleet was reduced by 11 percent. Then the shooting stopped.

By that time, Shanga's diminished squadron had made two more runs against the *Falcon*, losing another fighter. With Vuffi Raa at the controls, the freighter had gradually drawn them nearer where the fleet was busily destroying itself. Fire leaped here and there, lighting up the eternal night. Navy fighters blew up, showering their mother vessels with debris, spreading damage further. The oswaft darted in and out, their numbers very slightly diminished, too, as the sentients grew tired or careless.

Aboard the *Falcon*, Lando bore down on the quadgun once again, turning a small spacecraft into drifting junk.

"Say, that wasn't one of our bandits! That was a navy fighter. Where the Core are we, Vuffi Raa?"

From the control room, the robot replied, *"Entering the zone of conflict between the oswaft and the fleet. I'll try to keep us clear of any large ships, since we—There! Got another one!—since we can't maneuver like the spacepeople."*

A cluster of fighters swooped past the *Falcon*, ignoring her while blasting toward a cruiser that was breaking up. Three oswaft, concentrating all their power, had done that when one of her shields was down momentarily, due to a collision with a fighter.

Suddenly, Shanga's men were back, diving on the *Falcon* in turns, drawing her fire, getting in shots of their own. There was only one of Lando, and his arms were getting weary from their constant work at the quad-guns. The *Falcon* looped and soared, outmaneuvering the fighters again and again. Weapons flared, men died.

Without warning, all action ceased among the fleet. The blast and brilliance of shooting stopped as if someone had turned a switch. Every fighter was recalled.

At the center of things now, Lando and Vuffi Raa and Lehesu watched as a broad corridor was cleared among the ships. Shields up, they were immune to the oswaft, and, as long as they didn't fire on the vacuum-breathers, they suffered no more losses.

"Something on the scope, Master."

"Keep me advised."

Through the space cleared by the fleet, an older-model Centrality cruiser became visible, surface-coated dead black, bristling with an array of unfamiliar equipment. On its underside were emblazoned the arms of the Central Administrator himself. On its sides were added the ship's name:

WENNIS

"—by edict! You are commanded to cease fire and to surrender to the nearest Centrality vessel immediately."

Apparently, Vuffi Raa had found the navy's frequency—or they had found the *Falcon*'s and had patched it through the intercom. As he listened, Lando saw one of his auxiliary target screens go momentarily blank, then fill with the dark and terrifyingly familiar image.

"This in the name of the Central Administrator, the Council, and the People of the Centrality, at the order of Rokur Gepta, Sorcerer of Tund."

And then: "*Private to Captain Lando Calrissian of the* Millennium Falcon." The wizard leaned conspiratorially into the pickup. "*You have put up a valiant and brilliantly conceived fight, sir, but one which you shall inevitably lose, if only because I am willing to throw half the resources of civilization at you, should it prove necessary. I could bury you with dead Centrality bodies, and fill this entire nebula with the wrecks of ships, and I will.*

"*However, I offer you an opportunity to minimize unnecessary bloodshed, to settle things personally and at close hand between ourselves, once and for all. Nor have I need for the resources of half an empire to persuade you. At this very moment the power is mine to exterminate every sentient being in this nebula, every flyspeck of life, every hope that life again will ever flourish here.*

"*Behold and bear witness!*"

He raised a hand, as if in a magician's gesture. Outside, from one of the ungainly projections on the hull of the *Wennis*, there was a faint, fast squirt of brilliant life. Instantly it streaked toward a cluster of gigantic oswaft who, since ceasing to fight, had been watching and listening. Sen and Fey were among them.

As the light point reached them, they began glowing a pale, sickly green and disappeared without a trace before their dying screams had faded. Whatever the weapon was, it could discriminate between real organic beings and the phony outlines Lando had taught them to create. Those remained like ghosts, hollow and insubstantial.

"*That, my dear Captain Calrissian, was a demonstration employing one times ten to the minus seventeeth of the power available to me. The object was an electromagnetic torpedo, scarcely larger than a filterable virus and programmed to self-destruct after it had done its work. Had it not been so, this area around us would*

♦ 164 ♦

contain no life by now, nor, within a week, would the entire nebula.

"I offer you, however, an alternative. Should you triumph, I shall go away, taking the entire fleet with me. Should I win, I shall release a thousand tons of this destructive agent in the ThonBoka.

"As for ourselves personally, we shall fight a duel to the death."

SEVENTEEN

"We have one advantage, Master."

Vuffi Raa had just returned from the *Wennis*, where, at Gepta's command, he had gone as Lando's second to receive the terms for the duel. Frost was turning into water on the little robot's chromium-plated body and dripping off onto the floor of the tiny airlock below the topside hatch.

"That's absolutely peachy, old go-between. Any little boost would be welcome, just now." He looked out through a viewport. On one side the *Falcon* was englobed by the Centrality navy, perhaps five hundred enormous capital ships.

From another port, he could see they were hemmed in by Klyn Shanga's squadron, what was left of it, in formation once again about the pinnace. The tractor field was off, and would have been invisible in any case, but the arrangement gave them an instant choice between two modes of movement.

Lando shook his head, and went on running down the long-form checklist, getting his best spacesuit up and ready for the coming conflict.

"Yes, Master. You'll recall he was the one responsible

for your winning me in the first place? Well, it was he, as well, who, well, supplied me to the *Ottdefa* Osuno Whett. He knows me rather well—and still believes that he can program me to betray you."

The gambler looked up, set the pair of vacuum gauntlets he'd been working on aside, and lit a cigar. Possibly his last. "How very interesting. And can he?"

"Not at all. What's even better is that he still believes me to be bound by my earlier programming. He thinks I cannot fight."

Lando grinned. "You know, I'm not sure I understand that, myself. But of course that's why he offered to let you help me out in this duel, to make up for his powers of magic, so he said."

The robot raised an affirmative tentacle. "What now remains is for us to plan what we will do once we're out there. Have you an idea?"

Lando drew a deep puff, let it out slowly, savoring it. "I do, indeed, old Saturday-night spatial. The terms are one personal weapon apiece?"

"Not precisely, Master. You are allowed one weapon, I am allowed none. He didn't specify what he would use. I didn't ask. It seems we have no choice in this matter."

"No, but tell me, does he know about the way you let your tentacles do their own thinking?"

The gleam in Vuffi Raa's faceted eye grew brighter. "No, Master, I don't believe he does."

"Swell. Then here's what we'll do—and don't call me master."

Rokur Gepta stood in an airlock of the *Wennis*, watching the *Millennium Falcon* through the bull's-eye in the hatch. He could see her captain and his droid climbing out of their own airlock as he himself suited up. The suit was a deep nonreflective gray, about the color of the walls of the ThonBoka. He turned to the officer beside him, the nominal captain of the cruiser.

"You are certain that you understand my instructions?"

"Yes, sir," the unhappy-looking man replied. "I am to exterminate all life in the nebula, regardless of the outcome of the duel." He gulped at speaking what he felt to be a dishonorable and unmilitary decision, and remained rigidly at attention as the sorcerer donned his helmet.

"Precisely, Captain, and if you are entertaining any ideas of countermanding that order in the event of my demise, please remember that the continued existence of your family depends on its being carried out. That was the purpose of sending the courier to your home system a few minutes ago. Their lives are in your hands."

"Yes, sir."

"Very well, then, stand aside so that I may exhaust the lock—unless you care to join me in the airless void?"

Klyn Shanga watched the accursed Vuffi Raa, Butcher of Renatasia, climb out of the airlock of the *Millennium Falcon*. The little monster was still wearing that spacesuit he'd affected in the Oseon that made him appear to be a robot. Shanga began flipping switches; turbines whined as power levels increased. One trembling hand remained on the button of his weapon system. Steady, old soldier, he told himself, only a few more minutes.

Suddenly, a fighter across the formation from him slid forward, gaining speed as it approached the *Falcon*. Shanga opened his mouth to scream "Bern, no!" when a man-thick power beam from the *Wennis* struck fighter number Twenty-three, blowing it to bits.

"*Sorry, Admiral Shanga,*" a voice said over the intership. "*Orders from the Sorcerer of Tund. There is to be no interference.*"

And no revenge, no justice, Shanga realized, unless he could figure out something quickly. Ten years of his life, of the lives of all his men, down the drain, unless—

Movement near the *Wennis* caught his eye. Rokur Gepta jetted from the airlock, crossed half the space between the cruiser and the freighter, and came to a skillful hovering stop. He folded his spacesuited arms and hung, awaiting his adversaries. Across the void that had become an arena, Lando Calrissian followed his example in a bright yellow spacesuit, rocketing to meet the sorcerer, stopping several dozen meters away. Vuffi Raa was right behind him.

Something of the order of a billion pairs of eyes—or equivalent sensory equipment—watched as the sorcerer inclined his head in a small, grudging bow. Without further warning, his right hand lashed out, and a beam of energy struck the place where Lando—

—had been. He tumbled, spun, and recovered, something small and glittering in his own hand, but didn't return fire. Soaring, he made a complicated figure in the vacuum as Gepta fired twice more, missing both times. While the sorcerer was thus distracted, Vuffi Raa circled warily, working his way behind the gray-clad figure. Two more shots, then Gepta realized that he was being deceived. He whirled, just as the robot's tentacles separated from his pentagonal body, spreading, encircling the sorcerer's position, and moving in.

Almost hysterically, Gepta tried to burn the tentacles, but they wriggled and squirmed as they came toward him, each limb no longer where it had been when the aim was taken. Closer they came, closer.

Lando *fired*! striking Gepta squarely in the back. Incredibly, the stingbeam's energy passed through the sorcerer harmlessly, nearly striking Vuffi Raa's body, which was backing, slowly, clumsily away from the fight while it directed the tentacles to the attack.

Gepta whirled again, getting off three shots at the gambler. The last one hit him in the foot. There was a puff of steam and a hissing audible only to Lando, then the suit sealed, its medical processes already shutting off the pain. He had no idea how badly he'd been hurt, but he knew that he could still fight. He fired a second of his five shots, again taking the sorcerer in the center of the torso. Again the beam sliced through without apparent damage.

Then a tentacle grasped Gepta around the neck.

The gray-suited figure struggled, trying to unwrap the chromium-plated limb, but it hung on grimly. From his vantage pount in the squadron, Klyn Shanga watched, then was suddenly struck blind by a thought:

Vuffi Raa, so-called Butcher of Renatasia, really was a robot!

Nothing else could explain the independent limbs. But if that was true, then what of their mission of revenge? What of the only purpose they had had for living, since the death of their civilization. What of—"

Abruptly, there was a surge of motion as the tenuous hold of tractors at a hundredth power was broken and the pinnace moved forward of its own accord, leaving the fighters behind. No one aboard the vessels of the fleet seemed to notice, so much of their attention was riveted on the duel.

But Shanga did.

"What's going on, there? Who's in the pinnace?"

"*It is I, the* Ottdefa *Osuno Whett*," came the electronic reply. "*I'm going to end this farce, destroy the robot and the gambler—and perhaps Rokur Gepta, in the bargain! None of them are fit to—*"

Another blinding flash of recognition. It was the voice

that did it, separated now from the assumed appearance. Whett was the Butcher's aide! Whett was the Butcher's assistant! Whett was—

—the Butcher himself! It *had* to be! No other explanation was possible.

Heeling his fighter over, Klyn Shanga thumbed his weapons at the pinnace. The larger vessel's shields were up, however, shields designed to protect an admiral's tender person during ship-to-ship and ship-to-planet transfers. Shanga's fire coruscated off the invisible barrier.

"This is Zero Leader!" he shouted on the squadron's frequency. "Get that pinnace—the man we seek is aboard! I'll explain later, if we live!" Desperately, he punched buttons on the remote console that had controlled the pinnace on the trip out. He couldn't prevent Whett from driving it, nor drop its shields, but he could keep it out of hyperdrive and lock the tractor field.

He did the latter. The squadron snapped into formation. Opening his small ship's engines all the way, he screamed at his men to do the same. Slowly, inexorably, the assemblage of ships achieved headway.

Abruptly, someone aboard the *Wennis* noticed the motion.

"*Zero leader, this is the* Wennis! *Halt immediately, or we'll blast you out of the nebula!*" The warning was repeated. Gathering speed now, Shanga steered his squadron and their captive—who was desperately and ineffectually attempting to reverse things from the pinnace—toward the decommissioned cruiser. Faster and faster, skirting the space where the battle between Gepta and Lando and Vuffi Raa still raged, they zeroed in on the larger vessel.

A broad beam of power struck the pinnace squarely on the bow. Her shields held, and the energy, sluicing off the deflectors, missed the lightly shielded fighters as well. As they came within a few hundred meters of the *Wennis*, Shanga abruptly cast off the tractor field and flipped his craft around. Years of reflex allowed his men to follow the motion like a school of fish.

The pinnace struck the *Wennis*—her own shields negligently still powered down to allow the sorcerer to debark—and penetrated her hull. There was a brief instant in which nothing else happened, a suspension of time as inertia was overcome, as systems attempted to control the damage and failed.

Then a titanic explosion as the cruiser belched flaming gases everywhere, consuming herself, the pinnace, and everyone aboard both vessels. Even two of the fleeing fighters were tumbled badly.

Farther away, Rokur Gepta, Vuffi Raa, and Lando were distracted by the explosion. Gepta stared insanely. Lando recovered first, took aim, and—

—was struck by a piece of flying debris. His shot went wild, hitting the sorcerer in the ankle. In shock, Lando recovered and watched as the form of Rokur Gepta withered and faded. He jetted up beside the magician in time to see a heavy military blaster swing around, fire, swing a little farther, and fire again. Vuffi Raa's tentacle floated emptily with nothing left to hold onto. The third shot, cast by an unconscious and dematerializing hand, caught the robot's torso, a hundred meters away, dead in the center.

The metal glowed momentarily. When the incandescence dimmed, so had the single red eye in the body's center. It was flat, glassy, and black.

Lando pawed through Rokur Gepta's empty spacesuit. Down in the leg was a small bundle of ugly, slimy tissue, resembling a half-cooked snail, an escargot with a dozen skinny, hairy black legs. It was one of the most disgusting things the gambler had ever seen, but he'd seen it before.

It was a Croke, from a small, nasty system he'd once visited. The species was intelligent and unvaryingly vicious, and they were all masters of camouflage and illusion.

This one wasn't quite dead. The suit had protected it, and it was nearly impervious to hard vacuum. Lando ripped the suit away, took the stunned and putrid creature that had been Rokur Gepta, and *squeezed*. When he was through, his suit gloves were covered with greasy slime, but no Sorcerer of Tund would ever rule the galaxy.

As if Gepta's death were a signal, the Centrality fleet began to open up on the oswaft within range. In the space of a moment, hundreds died...until the fleet had other things to think about: Klyn Shanga's squadron was shooting back, giving the vacuum-breathing sentients covering fire so they could retreat. One fighter exploded, then another, but they were saving oswaft lives.

"CEASE FIRE IMMEDIATELY OR BE DESTROYED!"

The voice came over everybody's communicators simultaneously, at every frequency. Lando looked up from his little friend's scorched torso—he'd gathered in the tentacles, as well, but they would not attach themselves and lay in his arms like so many dead pieces of jointed metal—to see a figure that dwarfed the departed Elders, even the largest dreadnaughts in the Centrality fleet.

It was a starship, but it was at least fifty kilometers in diameter, a smooth, featureless, highly polished ovoid of silvery metal. Another, identical monster followed close behind it. Far to the rear, Lando watched as others, countless others, penetrated the supposedly impenetrable wall of the ThonBoka as if it were so much fog. Hundreds, thousands, hundreds of thousands.

Some fool aboard the *Recalcitrant* opened fire with

the new meter-thick destructor beam, deep green and hungry. A red beam from the leading foreign ship met the green one squarely, forced it back a meter at a time until it reached the navy cruiser. A pause, then the *Recalcitrant* became a cloud of incandescent gas.

"CEASE FIRE OR BE DESTROYED! THERE WILL BE NO SECOND WARNING!"

Racked with grief, Lando watched as more and more of the titanic ovoids appeared in the nebula. There was no way to estimate their number. The gambler thought they might fill up the Starcave, twelve light-years across as it might be.

Then a sensation brushed past him. Somehow he knew that only he could hear the tightly beamed message that issued from his helmet phones.

"You are Captain Calrissian, are you not. You have fought valiantly, and not in vain. You grieve for your little friend. I grieve, too, for he was my only son."

EIGHTEEN

"*Sabacc!*" said the One. "By the Center of Everything, Lando, I knew we would learn new and valuable things if only we dared to."

"Yeah, well, you've still got to learn the difference between luck and skill. That's eighteen trillion I'm ahead of you already, counting that last hand, and I don't even know yet what we're using for currency!"

The gambler took a deep drag on his cigar and watched as the One gathered in the seventy-eight-card deck with a sweep of a jointed metallic tentacle. His eye glowed a deep scarlet with delight and anticipation as he dealt them out again, two to Lando, two more to Klyn Shanga, two to the extensor manifesting itself as the Other.

"Too bad," he continued. "This game is a whole lot faster and more interesting five-handed. If only Vuffi Raa..."

"Each of us," observed the other, "sets his own course through the universe and must follow it where it takes us. This is called integrity, and to deviate—"

"Come on, you five-legged clowns, cut the pop philosophy and play cards! You know how long it's been since I sat down at a real table and—"

Lando grinned. "And tried filling inside straights all night long, Admiral? At that, it beats dodging bullets and destructor beams. I'm glad you decided to be on our side, and I'm especially glad you're a better fighter pilot than you are a *sabacc* player."

"I'm only warming up. Give me a chance, and I'll have your hide the easy way: payable in cash!"

Laughter around the table. It was good to have the lounge full of visitors, the gambler thought; a real passenger lounge for a change. But some folks seemed to be missing from his life, missing from places they'd carved for themselves only recently. Or relatively recently.

"Heard from Lehesu yet?" he asked, watching a Commander of Flasks change itself into a Three of Staves. He knew it was an electronic trick, but it never failed to give him goosebumps. Shanga was frowning, a sure sign he had a good hand, Lando had learned quickly. He kept his betting light.

The fighter pilot shook his head, still frowning. "One of the boys said something about seeing a middle-sized oswaft zooming off during the battle. Said something about a courier he wanted to catch up with. It is true the spacepeople want to make him High Supreme Galootie or something?"

A mechanical chuckle issued from the extensor representing the One. "It would seem they have decided that leadership—or at least wisdom—do not necessarily correlate positively with age. This is gratifying to me, as I am the youngest of my people...that is, I was before Vuffi Raa...er, I believe I shall take another card, gentlebeings."

Outside, far away across the Starcave, the actual repositories of the intelligence of the One, the Other, and the Rest lay, as it were, at anchor. They were gigantic fifty-kilometer starships, intergalactically self-propelled droids of ancient origin.

Shanga changed the subject. "I never quite got who it was who built you folks originally—that is, if you don't mind me asking a religious question."

"Not at all," the One replied. "They were a race of individuals who looked rather like these extensors. There are some among us who recall them, although I do not, except through cybernetically handed-down memories. They were not spacefarers; the idea simply didn't appeal to them. They were wiped out in a radiation storm when a nearby star went supernova. Only a few intelligent machines were left, and they were my ancestors. We did explore the stars, at least in our arm. There is a high incidence of unstable stars there, so that organic life is rare."

"Yes," the Other concurred, "it was his idea to seek out organic life to liven up our own culture, and here we are."

Lando shook his head. He wished his little robot friend were there to see this hand; it was a lulu. "Yes, but first you sent out an explorer whose memories were suppressed and who could not act violently. That way he'd generate fresh impressions and not get your civilization into trouble with others unless it was absolutely necessary."

"Correct," the One said. "And while the suppression worked, the conditioning did not. Self-preservation is a powerful motive, even though in the end—*sabacc!*"

"Beginner's luck!" the professional gambler howled, wondering how much he'd lost this time. He heard footsteps behind him, turned and looked down the curving corridor toward the engine area. A figure stood there, covered with grease, a spanner in one of its hands. Its five-sided carapace was still scorched.

"I got the deflectors readjusted, Master," Vuffi Raa said. "Admiral Shanga's men are good shots, but that weakness won't show up again now!"

"Fine. Now will you please stop being dutiful and join the game? And don't call me master in front of your old man, here, it's embarrassing."

Hours later, two days after the battle and departure of the fleet, Lando was dozing in his pilot's chair in the cockpit. Vuffi Raa was out somewhere, visiting his kinfolk.

"Captainmasterlandocalrissiansir, I have returned," the ship-to-ship said.

"Zzzzz—what? Lehesu! Why so formal all of a sudden—and where the Core have you been?" The gambler had heard it suggested that the young oswaft had run away from defending the ThonBoka. He didn't believe it for a moment, but he was curious.

"Oh, just before your duel with Rokur Gepta, I heard him tell an officer—his helmet microphone was open, apparently—that he was sending a courier to have that person's family murdered should he disobey a rather ugly order. I hopped after him, but it took me a while to catch up."

Lando stretched, yawned, reached for a cigar. "Oh? What did you do then, ask him to stop politely?"

"Why yes, and he did. In several pieces, I'm afraid: I shouted it at him."

The gambler chuckled. "So now you're home and going to be the Elder of all you survey, is that how it is?"

There was a long pause. *"No, not precisely. I told them I would not be their Elder, and if they wanted my advice, they wouldn't appoint a new one. I don't think they listened to me. I wish neither to give nor receive orders—something I learned from you, Lando my friend."*

Lando his friend scratched his head, a gesture he'd never had habitually until he'd picked it up from Vuffi Raa. "I'm glad to hear it. What are you going to do with yourself, then?"

"Explore, discover the answers to questions. Probably get in trouble again. But tell me, I am very confused on one point: the Millennium Falcon *is not really a person, is that correct? Nor the cruiser* Wennis?"

"The late, unlamented cruiser *Wennis*. I don't know what that life-destroying stuff was Gepta spewed around, but I'm glad it was destroyed with her. No, friend Lehesu, much as we may love her, the *Falcon* is a machine." He puffed on his cigar, anticipating the oswaft's next bewildered question. "And before you ask, yes, the One, the Other, and the Rest are indeed persons, of the mechanical persuasion. They think for themselves, the *Falcon* doesn't. In a sense, they are to you what Vuffi Raa is to me: you both live in free space; it's your natural environment. Vuffi Raa and I are arms-and-legs types, born and bred in a gravity well and most comfortable where there's light and heat and atmosphere."

"But Lando, what is *Vuffi Raa?"*

"A larval starship, if you believe him. The organic people who invented his ancestors looked like him, built machines that looked like him—the same idea as a humanoid robot. Today his people use 'extensors'—manipulators—that still look like him. If he's a good little bot and eats all his spinach, he'll grow up to be a starship, too. If he wants to."

Concern tinged the vacuum-breather's transmission. *"I'm told that he was nearly killed while I was gone. I feel somewhat guilty for—"*

"Forget it, old jellyfish, his daddy repaired him in just a few hours. What counts is the memory, the experiences, the character, and they were all intact, protected in googolicate at the deepest levels of his being. No little blaster was going to do more than freeze him up mechanically."

"What will you do now, Lando?"

"Well, I think it's time I gave up this wandering life, if only for a while. I need to do something responsible, own something, have some obligations. I'll think about it. I've learned a lot, and I have plenty to get started on. The Falcon's holds are full of gigantic gemstones—every variety I've ever seen or heard of, and a few I'm going to have to consult experts on. I could buy an entire city."

"And Vuffi Raa?"

"I don't know, old manta, I don't know."

The *Millennium Falcon*'s engines thrummed with pent-up energy. She was eager to go back into intergalactic space, eager for another adventure. In her cockpit, Vuffi Raa was finishing up a lecture: "And be sure to back the engines off at least three percent when initiating the deflector shields, otherwise the surge will overload her, and—"

"I know, I know, I know," her captain replied patiently while trying to suppress tears. "The only thing I don't understand is why you're going back this very minute. Why can't you—"

"Master, it is a bargain I have made. I would much prefer, like you and Lehesu, to continue exploring the universe, to have adventure and savor life. I will again, someday. But I was constructed for the purpose of recording those experiences and relaying them to my people. I feel the need to do this, as you feel the need to breathe. Do you understand, Master?"

"I understand." He patted the little droid's shiny torso. The rest of the blast damage had healed, and the robot looked as new and perfect as the day they'd met. "Well, if you ever get back to this arm of the galaxy, you know how to find me, don't you? I haven't much in the way of a permanent address."

There was an electronic chuckle. "I'll just go where there's the most trouble and noise, and there'll you be, Master."

"Not on your life! I'm going to settle down, be responsible. And Vuffi Raa?"

"Yes, Master?"

"Don't you think, now that you know exactly who and what you are, that you could stop calling me master?"

"Why, I suppose so, Lando. Why didn't you ask me before?"

ABOUT THE AUTHOR

Self-defense consultant and former police reservist, L. Neil Smith has also worked as a gunsmith and a professional musician. Born in Denver in 1946, he traveled widely as an Air Force "brat," growing up in a dozen regions of the United States and Canada. In 1964, he returned home to study philosophy, psychology, and anthropology, and wound up with what he refers to as perhaps the lowest grade-point average in the history of Colorado State University.

L. Neil Smith's previous books—all published by Ballantine/Del Rey—are *The Probability Broach*, *The Venus Belt*, *Their Majesties' Bucketeers*, *The Nagasaki Vector*, *Lando Calrissian and the Mindharp of Sharu*, and *Lando Calrissian and the Flamewind of Oseon*.